MW00829826

By Ramona Gray

Chapter 1

"Ms. Jones! My office, immediately."

His voice, harsh and demanding, spilled out of his office and I sighed before standing up from my desk. Smoothing my skirt, I entered his office and smiled at my boss.

"Is there a problem, Mr. Wright?"

"Shut the door," he barked.

I shut the door and sat down in one of the leather chairs across from his desk. I crossed my legs delicately and his eyes drifted to my short hemline before he glared at me.

"As a matter of fact, there is a problem. A rather large one."

I pasted my best 'what can I do to help' look on my face and folded my hands in my lap.

He raked his hand through his hair before his gaze dropped to my chest. "Your outfit, Ms. Jones."

My cheeks flamed immediately and I pulled self-consciously at my too-tight blouse. "Wh-what do you mean?"

"You know exactly what I mean, Ms. Jones." He leaned forward and folded his own hands on the top of his desk. "It isn't work appropriate. What do you have to say for yourself?"

"Laundry day," I whispered.

He frowned. "What?"

"It was laundry day yesterday and I didn't have any quarters for the washing machine." I cleared my throat nervously. "I didn't have anything else to wear."

I was nearly sweating with embarrassment. I had hemmed and hawed over my outfit this morning for half an hour but, left without much choice, had decided to just go for it. I knew what I looked like. The shirt was much too tight. It hugged my large breasts and clung to my curves and the skirt, well let's just say that bending over was not an option.

"How long have you worked for me, Ms. Jones?"

"Three years."

"I would think that after three years you'd have a better understanding of the office dress policy. Wouldn't you?"

My temper flared and I scowled at him. "I'm not breaking any rules. My skirt is well within the regulation length."

He scowled back. "Is it? Then explain why I got an eyeful of your garters when I walked by your desk. And I'll bet you a thousand dollars that the first deep breath you take, your buttons on that shirt pop open. Showing your tits is a definite infraction, Ms. Jones."

I gaped at him. "Did you just talk about my tits?"

He sat back in his chair and I watched wide-eyed as his hands moved to the buckle of his belt. "As I was saying, you've created a large problem and it's up to you to solve it."

As he was speaking, his hands were unbuckling, unbuttoning and unzipping.

A small gasp escaped my throat when he tugged his cock through the opening in his pants. It was long and thick and hard as a rock, and my mouth dried up as I watched him stroke it firmly.

"Come here and solve the problem, Ms. Jones," he commanded.

Like a woman in a dream, I rose to my feet and crossed around his desk. I couldn't take my eyes off of his cock and as moisture dampened my panties, I unconsciously rubbed my thighs together in an effort to quell the throbbing that was starting between my legs.

"On your knees, Ms. Jones." He rolled back his chair and I knelt obediently between his legs.

My mouth was in front of his cock now and I watched his hand slide up and down before he wound his other hand in my hair and pushed me toward the head of his cock.

"Open," he said firmly.

I opened my mouth and moaned in sheer delight when he guided his cock past my lips. I closed my mouth around his throbbing length, my stomach tightening with pleasure when I heard his harsh moan.

"Good girl," he whispered. He petted and stroked my hair as I sucked enthusiastically. His hips were rising in his chair and he was thrusting more firmly into my mouth. I made a soft humming noise and he groaned again before pulling on my hair.

"All of it. I want you to take all of it." He pushed on the back of my head and I took a deep breath and –

"Lina! Earth to Lina!"

I jerked and nearly fell off the stool I was sitting on. My hand twitched and the salad tumbled off my fork and landed with a wet splat on my shirt. I cursed loudly and mopped at the salad dressing with my napkin.

"What the hell were you thinking about, Lina?" My co-worker, Amanda, bit into her sandwich and stared curiously at me.

I blushed and continued to dab at the stain. "Nothing. Why?"

"You had a weird look on your face."

I shrugged. "I'm just tired. I didn't sleep well last night. Rex still isn't doing well and I was up half the night with him."

Amanda gave me a look of sympathy. "I'm sorry. I know how much he means to you."

"Thanks." I smiled at her and then glanced at the clock. "Shit. I've got to get back to my desk. Mr. Wright left a ton of documents for me before he went to his meeting. If I don't have them finished by the time he gets back, he'll have my head."

Amanda rolled her eyes. "I have no idea how or why you put up with him. He's an asshole."

I shrugged. "I need the money. It's not like there are a ton of jobs out there right now."

"I'd rather work at McDonalds then be his assistant," Amanda replied. "Do you know that before you, he went through seven assistants in just as many months? It was a bloodbath. I mean, we knew it would be difficult when Helen retired but seriously, we had no idea. The one girl had a nervous breakdown at her desk and Fran had to drive her home."

I laughed. "He's not that bad."

Amanda raised her eyebrow and I nodded in defeat. "Fine. He's that bad."

"Handsome bastard, though," Amanda said thoughtfully.

A snippet of my daydream reared its ugly head and I closed my eyes briefly before clearing my throat. "I hadn't noticed."

"Bullshit," Amanda scoffed.

"Fine. I've noticed. But honestly, he's such a douchebag that he isn't handsome to me anymore." There was no way in hell I would ever, even under the threat of hot needles being poked under my nails, admit to my crush on my asshole boss.

I slid off the stool and pulled nervously at my top and skirt. "Hey, Amanda? What do you uh, think of my outfit today?"

Amanda eyed me critically. "You look good. Different, but good." She hesitated. "Your shirt might be a teensy too tight for the office."

"Yeah," I sighed. "It's laundry day."

Amanda laughed and popped a grape into her mouth. "I overheard Gary and Marvin discussing your breasts by the photocopier machine. Gary thinks you're a D cup but Marvin is confident you're a double D."

"Fucking perverts," I muttered.

"They sure are," Amanda agreed cheerfully. "So, which is it? D or double D?"

I stuck my tongue out at her. "None of your business, Pervey McPerve."

She laughed again. "You should have seen the looks on their faces when they turned around and saw Mr. Wright standing behind them."

I groaned. "Please tell me he didn't overhear them."

"Of course he did. He gave them that look - you know the one - and told them if they had enough time to discuss their co-worker's assets over the water cooler, then he obviously wasn't giving them enough clients. Next thing you know, they're both buried in files."

She snorted laughter as I tugged again at my top and left the lunch room.

* * *

I sighed wearily and rubbed my aching back before bending over the filing cabinet in Mr. Wright's office. It was close to seven and I was tired and hungry. The building was empty and I kicked off my shoes as I stuffed files back into the cabinet.

Technically I didn't have to work late, Mr. Wright hadn't even returned to the office this afternoon, but my day tomorrow would be much smoother if I did. Besides, I wanted to leave a little early tomorrow. Rex had yet another vet appointment and it would be much easier to get Mr. Wright to agree if I was caught up on my work.

I glanced around his office as I grabbed another file folder. I hated being in here. It smelled like him, like the expensive cologne he always wore, and I swear to God some days I could smell it even at my apartment. Not surprising. Most days I spent more time in here than I did at my own desk. Of course his cologne would linger on me.

I grabbed another folder and bent over the filing cabinet again. I was just sliding it into its proper spot when his low voice spoke directly behind me.

"Working late, Ms. Jones?"

I yelped in surprise and straightened, my hands rushing to pull my skirt into a more appropriate position. He was so close I could feel his breath on the back of my neck, and I twitched in surprise when I felt his erection brush against my ass.

"No, don't." His hands pulled mine away from my skirt and I gasped when he let his fingers stroke my nylon-clad thigh. "You didn't strike me as a garters and thong kind of girl, Ms. Jones."

"I – a girl has to have a few surprises, Mr. Wright," I squeaked out.

"Indeed. Go on, finish your filing," he instructed.

Holding the folder between my suddenly sweaty fingers, I tried to move past him. He made a noise of disapproval and his hands curled around my waist. "I think you can reach it from here, Ms. Jones."

I took a deep breath and bent over, stretching to put the folder away as his hands moved from my waist to my hips. My skirt was riding up and he helped it along with a few firm tugs. I moaned quietly when his hard hands stroked my ass and his finger tugged at the silk between my cheeks.

"Your skirt is much too short for the office, Ms. Jones. You're not setting a very good example for the other secretaries," he chided sternly as his hands continued to rub and caress.

"I'm sorry," I moaned.

"I don't believe you. I think you wore this skirt on purpose. I think you want me to punish you," he said silkily.

"Mr. Wright, I – "

His hand came down, smacking my backside sharply and I let out a squeal of protest.

"Quiet, Ms. Jones. Take your punishment like a good girl." His hand was sliding into my hair and when he pulled my head up and licked my throat, I thrust my ass against him. He spanked me again and I bit back my gasp of pain.

"Open your legs, Ms. Jones." His hand tightened in my hair and I parted my legs eagerly. His hand cupped me through the silk and I moaned loudly.

"You're not to enjoy this. Do you understand?" He said sternly.

"Yes," I whispered.

His fingers were working their way under my panties. "If you come, your punishment will be even more severe. Is that what you want?"

"No," I moaned. His fingers were almost there, they were nearly touching me and knowing that he would feel how wet I was only excited me more. I spread my legs wider and held my breath. If he didn't touch me, I would –

"Ms. Jones?"

I gave a startled shriek and straightened before whirling around. The object of my sexual fantasies was standing in the doorway of his office and, blushing furiously, I yanked my skirt down.

Oh God. I had just flashed my boss. There was no way in hell he hadn't seen my super-sized ass in my too-short skirt and while that might have been a-okay in my fantasies, it most certainly was not in real life. The plain white cotton underwear I was wearing wasn't turning anyone on any time soon.

"What are you doing in my office?" He frowned at me as he strode toward his desk. He was still wearing his suit but he had loosened his tie and unbuttoned the first few buttons of his shirt.

"Filing."

"Obviously," he snapped. "I meant, why are you still here? It's late."

I shrugged. "I wanted to get it finished before I left."

"Your dedication to your job is admirable." There was a tone of sarcasm in his voice and I scowled at him.

"You know, most bosses would be impressed by their assistant's dedication."

"Indeed." He sank into his chair and pulled a glass and a bottle of scotch from the bottom drawer. "Or perhaps they would hope that their secretary was capable of getting her job done during regular working hours."

I bit back my smart-ass retort. I hated being called his secretary and the man knew it. It was a dated and ridiculous term and he used it solely to get under my skin. Normally I would call him on it but I still needed to leave early tomorrow.

I quickly filed the last folder and slipped into my shoes as he poured scotch into a glass. He opened his laptop and stared moodily at the screen as I approached his desk and cleared my throat.

"What is it, Ms. Jones?"

"I need to leave early tomorrow."

"For what purpose?" He gave me a sharp glance.

"I have an appointment."

He frowned at me. "You've had a lot of appointments as of late."

I didn't reply. I had never mentioned Rex to him. Mr. Wright didn't strike me as a dog lover and I wouldn't put it past him to deny my request just because he hated dogs.

He took a swallow of his scotch. "Fine."

"Thank you, Mr. Wright."

"Good night, Ms. Jones," he replied dismissively.

I rolled my eyes and closed his door before collapsing in the chair at my desk. I had worked for Aiden Wright for three years. Three years of putting up with his shit, his sarcasm, his crazy work demands. Three years of crying in the bathroom and watching my social life go down the drain because of my work schedule. I shook my head and collected my stuff before moving to the elevators. The other financial advisors gave their assistants flowers and took them for lunch on Administrative Assistant Day. They gave bonuses at Christmas and never called them in from their vacation because they needed a document typed. In the three years I had worked for him, Aiden Wright had never once given me a bonus or hell, even told me I was doing a good job. I was a fool to keep working for him.

So why are you? Find another job where you're not treated like dirt.

It was excellent advice and one that I would never follow. Some weird part of me liked the constant stress working for Aiden Wright caused. The thought of sitting in some office where my boss was always perfectly polite and perfectly reasonable, made me want to break out in hives. I hated to be bored and working for Mr. Wright was far from boring.

Whatever. You just keep hoping all your goddamn sexual fantasies about the man will come true someday.

My cheeks reddened and I stepped out of the elevator in a hurry. I crossed the lobby, my heels clicking loudly in the silence, and walked quickly to my car. It was freezing cold and I cursed loudly when I slipped and nearly landed on my ass.

The man is not attracted to fat girls. Get it through your head, you idiot.

I sighed and rubbed my hands together briskly as I waited for my car to warm up. Aiden Wright was sex on a stick. His dark hair and dark eyes, the sharp cheekbones and the perfect amount of stubble that always covered his jaw, made women drool. He worked out religiously every morning in the gym in the basement of our office building and at 6'4" he towered over nearly every one.

I sighed again and drove out of the parking lot. My fantasies about my boss had to stop. They had really heated up over the last few days and although part of me knew it was a coping mechanism for the stress, it was time to end them. Although I had never once seen Mr. Wright with a woman, I knew without a doubt that I wasn't his type. Besides, he was probably the type of guy who liked a woman to be in control in bed.

I snorted out loud as I drove carefully down the icy streets. That was complete and utter bullshit and I knew it. Mr. Wright was a man who demanded obedience and there was no reason to think he wouldn't be the same in the bedroom. Fresh wetness dampened my panties at the thought of being under his control and I groaned and slammed my hand against the steering wheel. I really needed to get laid.

Chapter 2

"Ms. Jones!"

His angry bellow had me leaping from my chair and scurrying into his office. "What's wrong?"

"Where the hell is maintenance?"

I could barely hear him over the rattling of the vent in his ceiling. "I've called them three times."

"Call them again!" He snarled. "How the hell am I supposed to get any work done?"

"They said they'd be here as soon as they can."

"As soon as they can?" He glared at me. "Do I need to do your job and call maintenance, Ms. Jones?"

"Go ahead!" I snapped. "I'm sure the owner of the company would have more pull than his assistant."

He stood up abruptly and stalked toward the door. "I'm going downstairs to get a coffee. You have ten minutes to get maintenance up here and fix this vent or I'll fire the whole lot of you. Do I make myself clear?"

"Perfectly," I replied as he stalked from the room.

I immediately hurried back to my desk and called maintenance, sighing impatiently when they didn't pick up the phone. Great, now they were avoiding my calls. I slammed my phone down and checked my watch. Eight minutes.

Grumbling to myself, I ran to the kitchen and grabbed a butter knife before hurrying back to Mr. Wright's office. I peered up at the vent. It rattled loudly and I slipped off my shoes and climbed on to his desk. I pried off the cover, shaking my head when bits of ceiling fell on to my face, and peered inside.

One of the metal pieces inside was vibrating loudly and, standing on my tiptoes, I strained to reach the screw with the butter knife. I could only just reach it and I cursed loudly when the knife just grazed the head of the screw. I moved closer to the edge of his desk, planting my toes at the very edge and made a soft grunt of triumph when I could reach the loose screw. I checked my watch. Two minutes. I twisted the butter knife, sweat breaking out on my forehead as I teetered a little on my toes.

"What the hell are you doing?"

I shrieked at the sound of his voice, my body jerking wildly and the butter knife falling from my hand as I slipped on his desk. I pinwheeled my arms madly but gravity was being a bitch and I fell straight into my boss. He grunted with surprise and staggered backward, tripping over the chair and falling flat on to his back as I landed on him with a heavy thud that made him wince. I barely felt the hot coffee soaking into my sweater as I scrambled off of him. I was mortified.

"I'm so sorry, Mr. Wright! Are you – are you okay?"

Please God, don't let me have crushed his ribcage. Please, sweet baby Jesus, I'm begging you.

He sat up and tossed his crushed coffee cup to the side. I could see a few splashes of coffee on his suit jacket but the majority of the coffee was soaking into my clothes and I grimaced and plucked at my sweater as he scowled at me.

"What the hell, Ms. Jones?"

"I'm so sorry," I whispered. My cheeks were flaming red and I wanted to sink into the floor. I stood up quickly. "Are you hurt? Do you need to go to the hospital?"

He climbed gracefully to his feet and scowled at me. "No, I'm not hurt. But thanks to your clumsiness, my coffee is – "

He stopped, noticing for the first time the large wet stain on my sweater, and cursed loudly. I squeaked in surprise when he took my wrist and nearly dragged me into his private bathroom.

"Take off your sweater!" He barked at me.

"What? No, I can't – "

With a harsh sigh of impatience, he grabbed the hem of my sweater and yanked it over my head. I was wearing a light pink shirt under it, and he quickly unbuttoned it as I stared at him in shocked silence. He peeled off my wet shirt and made another sigh of impatience at the sight of my camisole.

"How many layers are you wearing, Ms. Jones?"

"I get cold," I said defensively.

His hands reached for the bottom of my camisole and I slapped at his hands. "Hey, no! Don't do that!"

"It's covered in coffee and I need to see if you're burned," he said impatiently. He ignored my flailing hands and pulled my last layer over my head. I immediately crossed my arms over my breasts, acutely aware of the way my nipples were hardening in my bra, as he studied the redness of my upper chest.

"Shit," he muttered. He touched the reddening skin with the tips of his fingers and I jerked backward.

"It's fine," I replied. "It barely hurts."

He scowled at me. "Obviously that's not true."

I licked my lips nervously. It had nothing to do with the pain. His touch, the feel of his surprisingly rough fingertips tracing the sensitive skin of my chest, was what had made me jerk back. He'd never once touched me in the three years I had worked for him, not even an accidental brush, and my nerve endings were singing from just that brief contact.

He soaked a hand towel in cool water before pressing it against my chest. I hissed lightly at the cold and he frowned again.

"Take off your bra."

I gave him a startled look. "No."

"Take it off. Now, Ms. Jones."

My hands trembling, I reached for the front clasp and unhooked it. I shrugged it from my shoulders, letting it fall to the floor, as I closed my eyes.

He didn't say anything and after a moment, I opened my eyes and stared up at him. He was studying my breasts, and I thought I saw a glimmer of need in his dark eyes as a drop of water slid down my right breast and hovered on my erect nipple.

He bent his head and licked the drop of water from my nipple. I moaned, my heart beating like a drum in my chest, and my hands curled into his hair as he licked my nipple again and then sucked firmly on it.

He let the towel fall to the floor and cupped my left breast, kneading it with his strong hand as I arched my back and moaned encouragingly. His other hand slid around my back and as he pulled me against him I –

"Ms. Jones?"

"What?" I opened my eyes, dragging myself out of yet another sexual fantasy about my unsuspecting boss, and willed myself not to blush as he continued to press the wet towel against my chest.

"I think you should go to the hospital."

I shook my head. "No, it's fine. It's not burnt."

"You need to have it looked at." He glared at me.

"I don't," I insisted.

"What the hell were you doing on my desk anyway?" He asked.

"Fixing the vent," I muttered. "Maintenance is avoiding my calls and I only had ten minutes."

He rolled his eyes. "So you decided to fix it yourself? That doesn't seem wise, Ms. Jones."

"Yeah, well my boss isn't the most reasonable guy in the office," I shot back.

He snorted laughter before pressing the towel more firmly against my skin and I gave him a hesitant look.

"Are you okay? Maybe you should go to the hospital."

"For what?"

"I, um, landed pretty hard on you and I'm heavy. You've probably got a cracked rib," I muttered.

"Doubtful," he replied.

We stood there in silence for a few minutes until I couldn't stand it any longer. I reached for the towel. "I think I'm good. I'm sure you have work to do."

He gave me an irritated look as I tugged at the towel. "I still think you should go to the hospital."

"Well, I'm not," I said firmly. "Let go of the – "

I gasped when one of my hands touched his and my nerve endings sizzled and sang once more. I jerked my hands away, dropping the towel just as he relinquished his hold on it, and it fell to the floor with a wet plop. His eyes dropped to my large breasts and he stared for a long moment at my nipples straining against the lacy fabric of my bra.

I should have been folding my arms over my breasts but I couldn't. I was mesmerized by the look on his face. If I didn't know any better, I would swear it was lust. The thought that Aiden Wright would be lusting after me sent a shot of desire through my body and my nipples hardened further into tight, painful pebbles. He made a low sound in the back of his throat and I watched wide-eyed as his hand moved toward my breast. He was about to cup it when he took a step back and, without looking at me, stormed out of the small bathroom.

I released my breath in a harsh rush and rubbed at my forehead. What the fuck had just happened?

The door opened and Mr. Wright stuck his hand in. There was a shirt dangling from his fingers and he shook it impatiently at me. "Here, you can wear this."

"Th-thank you," I stuttered. I took the shirt and slipped into it. It was obviously one of his extra shirts and while it was a little tight across the breasts, it hung nearly to my knees. My heart thudding wildly, I gathered my clothes and stepped out into his office. He was sitting behind his desk, staring grimly at his laptop, and I took a few tentative steps toward him.

"I'll just finish fixing the vent," I began nervously.

"Leave it!" He snapped.

I nodded and nearly ran from his office.

* * *

"I'm sorry, Lina. There really isn't anything else we can do for him," Dr. Morrison said gently.

I stared down at Rex. He was lying on the floor of the examining room and he gave a weary sigh before closing his eyes.

"Are you sure?" I whispered.

"I am. You've done everything you can but he's an old dog. I think it's time to say goodbye."

The tears dripped down my face as Dr. Morrison patted my back gently before squatting and stroking Rex's fur. Rex didn't open his eyes and Dr. Morrison glanced up at me.

"It's the right decision, Lina."

I nodded, the lump in my throat prevented me from speaking, and Dr. Morrison patted Rex one last time before standing. "I'll be right back."

He squeezed my shoulder and left the room. I laid down on the floor beside Rex and stroked his head. He sighed again and I buried my face against him and let the tears soak into his soft fur.

"You're a good boy, Rexie," I whispered. "Mama loves you so much."

He chuffed softly but kept his eyes closed and I rubbed his grey muzzle and kissed the top of his head.

"I love you," I whispered again.

* * *

I stood in the middle of my living room and stared at Rex's empty bed. I was awake all night, staring at the bed where Rex used to sleep and trying to come to terms with the idea that I would never see him again. That I would never again hear his soft snoring or watch his tail wag furiously when I said the word 'walk'.

Tears streamed down my face and I sat down heavily on the couch and stared out the window at the falling snow. I had called in sick to work this morning. Mr. Wright would be furious with me. One of his largest clients was coming in tomorrow for an important meeting and their file wasn't completed but I couldn't bring myself to care. Ever since that moment in the bathroom last week, Mr. Wright had been an even bigger dick than usual. The thought of having to smile and nod and pretend my heart wasn't shattered into a million pieces as he yelled at me, was too much.

My cell phone rang and I stared at the familiar number of the office. Without answering it, I set it on the coffee table and headed back to my bed. I would worry about the office and Mr. Wright tomorrow.

* * *

"I am so glad you're back, Lina. Yesterday was a damn nightmare! I had to help Mr. Wright with his file and he was a complete and utter monster. I must have retyped the correspondence a million – "

Amanda trailed to a stop and studied my pale face carefully.

"Lina? Are you feeling better?"

"Yeah," I lied.

She frowned. "Tell me what's wrong."

I swallowed thickly and blinked back the tears. "Rex died."

"Oh, honey." Amanda hugged me tightly. "I'm so sorry."

"Thanks," I whispered.

"Do you want to talk about it?"

I shook my head. "No. I should get to work. What's left on the file to do?"

"Not that much. It shouldn't take you more than an hour or so." She squeezed my arm and I gave her a grateful smile.

"Thanks for helping out yesterday, Amanda. I know it wasn't pleasant."

"You're welcome, honey. Do you want to go for drinks after work tonight? We'll toast Rex's memory and then I'll be your wingman and get you laid."

I smiled a little. "I'll let you know, okay?"

"Okay." She hugged me again and we parted ways.

I sat down at my desk. The light was off in Mr. Wright's office, and I breathed a sigh of relief before going over Amanda's detailed notes. Nearly forty minutes later, I placed the documents on Mr. Wright's desk before heading to the kitchen for coffee.

When I returned, he was in his office and, steeling myself, I stuck my head into the room. "Good morning, Mr. Wright. Would you like a coffee?"

He stared icily at me. "Come in and shut the door, Ms. Jones."

I sighed and did as he asked.

Without looking up from the papers on his desk, he said, "You didn't answer your phone yesterday."

"I wasn't feeling well."

"You knew the file was due for today."

"I did," I acknowledged.

"I expect a certain standard from my employees. I can't have them staying home with a case of the sniffles when files are due," he said angrily.

"I knew Amanda could help you."

"Barely!" He finally looked up at me. "I thought you had a better work ethic than this. I'm disappointed in you, Ms. Jones."

Something inside of me snapped. Three years of listening to his shit, of putting up with his complaints and demands and never being good enough came rushing out of me like a runaway freight train.

"My dog died, you fucking asshole!" I shouted at him. "I didn't come to work yesterday because the night before I sat on the vet clinic floor and held my dog as he died! I'm so sorry that my grief over my dead dog was a hardship for you! I called in sick because I didn't feel like trying to explain the concept of grief to a cold-hearted, selfish, inconsiderate bastard like you!"

I clenched my hands into fists and glared at him. "I have spent the last three years of my fucking life trying to make you happy. I've missed family reunions and vacation trips, and my social life has gone down the fucking toilet all because of the insane hours you make me work. And you're going to sit there and question my goddamn work ethic? You're such an asshole! You never say thank you, you never acknowledge the work I do, hell you can't even spring for a lousy bunch of fucking flowers on Secretary's Day! You've got more money than God but you pay me so little that I can barely afford to pay my mortgage, and you wouldn't understand the idea of a bonus if it slapped you in the face."

He opened his mouth and I shook my head angrily. "No. I'm done. Do you hear me? I quit. Good luck finding someone else to put up with your shit!"

I flipped him the bird, turned on my heel and stormed out of his office.

Chapter 3

I was sitting on the couch Saturday morning, drinking a cup of tea and trying to come to terms with the fact that my dog was dead and I had quit my job in a truly spectacular fashion yesterday, when the doorbell rang. I peered through the peephole and took a step backward in surprise.

"What do you want?" I said through the door.

"Let me in, Ms. Jones."

"Why should I?"

"Please let me in, Lina."

My jaw dropped. Not once in three years had I ever heard my boss say my given name. It had been 'Ms. Jones' from day one. I ignored the little shiver that went down my spine and pasted a scowl on my face before opening the door.

"What do you want?"

"May I come in?" He asked.

"What for?" I replied rudely.

"I'd like to speak with you in private."

I hesitated and then shrugged. "Fine, whatever."

He followed me down the hall to the living room. I was acutely aware of my ripped t-shirt and yoga pants and I smoothed my hair self-consciously as I sat down on the couch.

He took off his jacket and gloves, laying them neatly in the armchair, and frowned at the look on my face. "What?"

"Nothing," I croaked. "You look weird in jeans."

He glanced down at his long-sleeved shirt and jeans as I tried to control my breathing. I had never seen him in anything but a suit before and it wasn't right that a man could look that good in a pair of jeans.

"Good weird or bad weird?" He asked politely.

"Just weird." I couldn't believe I was still lusting after my damn boss. Ex-boss, I amended.

He sat down in the armchair and said something so unexpected I could only stare at him.

"I'm sorry about your dog, Lina."

When I didn't reply he gave me a rueful look. "Contrary to popular belief, I'm not completely soulless and I happen to have a dog myself. I'd be devastated if he died."

I swallowed hard. "You have a dog?"

"I do. His name is King."

He glanced around my apartment before clearing his throat. "I also wanted to ask you to reconsider your decision about quitting."

"No," I replied immediately. "I'm done working for you."

He held up his hand. "Just listen to what I have to say, okay? If I promise to be more," he hesitated, "patient, would you consider coming back to work?"

I rolled my eyes. "It's impossible. You're permanently irritated and I don't want to deal with it anymore."

"I understand why you think that but I promise you I'll be better," he replied. "I had no idea that my behavior was affecting you so negatively."

"No idea?" I raised my eyebrows at him. "You're horrible to me. I mean, you're horrible to everyone, but you're the worst to me. I've cried in the bathroom at work, for God's sake. And do you have any clue how often I have to apologize for you? How often I've had to convince one of your employees not to quit? You have zero people skills, Mr. Wright. Zero."

"That's true. I don't give a shit what most people think of me and I can't really pretend to," he admitted.

I rolled my eyes again. "And that's why I'm not coming back to work for you."

"It's different with you, Ms. Jones."

"No, it isn't."

"It is," he said patiently. "Although I may not have admitted it in the past, you're the best damn sec – admin assistant – I've ever had. I need you."

Another shiver went down my spine. I liked the way it sounded when he said he needed me. Sure, he meant work, but there was no harm in pretending he meant it another way.

Plenty of harm, you moron. Stop letting your libido make your decisions for you.

"If I come back to work for you," I said slowly, "do I have your permission to tell you when you're being a complete asshat?"

"Yes," he said quickly. "Absolutely."

"And I want a raise. Five dollars more an hour."

"Done."

I took a deep breath. "I'll come back."

"Excellent." He stood and grabbed his jacket. "What are your plans for today, Ms. Jones?"

"I, um, nothing," I said in confusion.

"I have a cabin up in the mountains. I'm driving up there for the day, there are a few repairs I need to do, and I wondered if you'd like to join me?"

My mouth dropped open. "Are you asking me on a date, Mr. Wright?"

"Good God, no," he said so quickly that I blushed with embarrassment. "But you did happen to mention that you had no social life, thanks to me, and I thought you might enjoy getting out of the house for a bit. It's a nice drive and although the cabin is a bit rustic I think you'll like it."

"I don't think it's a good idea," I said softly. "It would look strange for the two of us to be um, hanging out together."

"Who's going to see us? The deer?" He asked impatiently. "Come, Ms. Jones. It's better than sitting in your house with bad memories."

When I continued to hesitate, he gave me his familiar look of exasperation. "This is me trying to be nice, Ms. Jones."

That made me laugh and I stood up. "Fine. I'll go. Give me ten minutes."

"Dress warmly," he advised as I headed out of the living room.

* * *

I climbed into the black SUV and settled into my seat. "So how long will it take to get there?"

I shrieked in surprise when a very large and very wet tongue licked the side of my face.

"King, down." Mr. Wright made a hand gesture at the giant dog leaning over my seat and King chuffed loudly before returning to his seat. I twisted and stared at the dog.

"What kind of dog is he?" I asked as King thumped his tail enthusiastically and a long string of drool dripped from his mouth to the leather seat.

"English Mastiff." Mr. Wright backed out of the driveway and headed down the street. "He's just over a year old and still a little excitable."

I wiped the drool from my cheek before reaching back and letting King sniff my hand. His tail sped up and he licked my fingers and chuffed again. I scratched the side of his face before turning in my seat and buckling my seat belt.

"How long will it take to get to the cabin?"

"A couple of hours," he replied.

"You don't seem like the cabin type to me, Mr. Wright."

He snorted. "Call me Aiden. And I'll have you know I'm very outdoorsy."

"Really?"

"Yes, really. I go on a hunting trip with my father every year, and I fish and camp during the summer."

He glanced at me as he turned on to the highway. "How about you? Are you outdoorsy?"

"I'm outdoorsy in that I like to get drunk on patios," I replied.

He snorted laughter and I grinned at him. "It's an enjoyable hobby, Aiden."

His name sounded foreign on my lips and I suppressed the lick of lust that went through me. It would be wiser to stick to Mr. Wright. Aiden felt much too intimate for me, considering the way I lusted after him.

"What was your dog's name?" He asked suddenly.

"Rex."

"What kind of dog was he?"

"Just a mutt. Mostly lab with some shepherd I think. I got him from the animal shelter when he was five. He'd been there for a few months. No one wants the plain, black dogs but I knew he was special the moment I saw him."

"Will you get another dog?" He asked.

"I don't know," I said softly.

I could feel the tears threatening and I cleared my throat roughly before looking out the window. I didn't want to cry in front of my boss, no matter how much he loved dogs.

"Did you dress warmly enough?" Aiden asked suddenly.

I nodded as he merged onto the highway leading out of the city. I could see the mountains rising in the distance and I smiled at Aiden when he gave me a dubious once-over.

"Are you sure? It really is a different kind of cold up there and – "

"I'm wearing my woollies," I interrupted.

He gave me a quizzical look and I leaned down and rolled up the leg of my jeans. I was wearing a pair of long underwear and he grinned as I pushed my jeans back down.

"I'm wearing thick socks and I've got two layers of shirts plus my hoodie and my jacket. And I have my toque, mittens and scarf in my bag."

"Good." He settled back in his seat and glanced curiously at me. "Am I really that terrible to work for, Lina?"

I didn't reply and he frowned. "Tell me the truth, Ms. Jones."

I sighed. "Yes, you are. You're rude and demanding and you never say thank you. And you hurt people's feelings all the time."

He scowled. "People are too sensitive."

"Maybe," I agreed. "But in an office environment you have to work with all sorts of different personality types."

"So being the boss doesn't give me an out?" He asked hopefully and I shook my head.

"No. In fact, being the boss means you need to set a good example to everyone of how to treat their coworkers," I lectured.

He sighed. "Why aren't you in HR? You'd fit right in with the rest of the happy hippies."

I laughed until tears ran down my face and King made an alarmed woof from the back seat. When I finally got myself under control, I glanced at my boss. He was grinning at me and I wondered how weird it would be if I snapped a picture of him with my cell phone. Super weird, I decided.

"Well, why aren't you in HR?" He repeated.

"Maybe I'm not a happy enough hippie," I teased.

He rolled his eyes. "You know what I mean. HR people are way too nice and happy for their own good."

"Actually," I mused, "people in HR usually burn out the fastest. It's a stressful job."

"Is that why you're not in HR?"

"Oh no, I would love to work in HR," I said enthusiastically. "In fact, about three years ago I had enrolled in one of the business colleges and was taking some HR courses in the evening. I loved it."

"Why did you stop?" He asked curiously.

I hesitated. One of the major reasons I had stopped was because I had lost my job with the law firm when they were forced to make cut-backs, and the position at Aiden's company was a much lower paying position. I had been a bit desperate though and even then Kent had been making noise about me not pulling my weight with rent and other bills. I had taken the job at Aiden's company and quit the night courses. A year later, Kent had dumped me and with mortgage and car payments, and daily expenses on my meager salary, I would never be able to afford to go back. Of course, I had just negotiated a pay raise.

"Lina?" Aiden prompted.

"It was too expensive," I said briefly.

He frowned but didn't say anything and I smiled cheerfully at him. "So, do you go up to your cabin every weekend?"

"I try to. It's nice to get away," he replied. "I bought it about four years ago and have been steadily fixing it up since then."

"You don't strike me as the 'Mr. Fix-It' type," I said honestly.

He laughed. "I like to work with my hands. When I was in university, I worked construction to pay for tuition."

"Really?"

He nodded. "Yeah, my parents couldn't afford to send me to university."

He smiled a little at my look of surprise. "Do I come across as a spoiled little rich boy?"

I shrugged. "You do have a strong 'I come from money' vibe."

"Good," he said arrogantly. "It's better for business."

I laughed. "You're just full of surprises today, Mr. Wright."

He grinned boyishly at me. "I do like to keep people on their toes, Ms. Jones."

Chapter 4

"Oh, wow. It's gorgeous," I breathed as I walked into the cabin. King bounded ahead of me and sniffed the entire place enthusiastically as I looked around curiously.

"It's not very big but I've made a lot of improvements to it," Aiden replied as I kicked off my boots.

"I love it!" I said enthusiastically.

"I thought you might." Aiden grinned as he moved to the fireplace and quickly built a fire. "Leave your jacket on until it warms up in here."

The cabin was small and cozy and I peered interestedly into the kitchen. The main area of the cabin was one open space with an island separating the kitchen from the living room, and I ran my hand along the smooth, granite surface.

"This is lovely."

"Thanks, I installed it myself," Aiden replied.

"Impressive."

"Actually, I gutted the entire kitchen and redid everything." He joined me and, as he pointed out the various improvements he had completed, I couldn't stop from smiling. He was like a kid in a candy store and before this moment, I would never have guessed that this version of my grumpy, rude boss even existed.

"This is the bathroom." Aiden opened a door to show me the small room. "There's no tub, just a shower, but there's plenty of hot water. And this," he led me to the second door, "is the bedroom."

I peered into the room. It was very small with just enough room for a double bed and a wooden dresser.

"It's nice."

He laughed. "It's small and absolutely freezing in the winter. Most nights I have to sleep on the pull-out couch in the living room. Eventually I'll open up the back wall and expand the cabin further out. I'll add a second fireplace and maybe even a second bedroom."

I gave him an admiring look. "You can do all that yourself?"

"Most of it. I'll have to hire some contractors for the second chimney and the electrical stuff. I have a friend, Joe, who lives about half a mile away. He's pretty handy and will help me with a lot of it.

"What is it you're going to do today?" I asked curiously.

"I need to work on the shed," he replied. "I'm putting in some shelving on the inside and I need to replace some of the boards on the outside. They're starting to rot. I should have done it in the fall but I was finishing up the kitchen."

He led me back into the living room. It had started to warm up and I shed my jacket as he pointed to a cupboard in the kitchen. "There's coffee, tea, and hot chocolate in that cupboard. Help yourself. I'm going to go out and start on the shelving in the shed. Feel free to just relax in front of the fire or have a nap on the couch. There are some books in the cabinet if you'd like to read."

I rummaged through my bag and pulled out my book. "I've got one, thank you." I smiled at him as he pulled a knitted cap off a hook on the wall.

"Well just shout at me if you need anything. Okay?"

"You bet."

He started toward the front door and turned around when I called his name hesitantly.

"Yes, Ms. Jones?"

"Thanks for this." I looked around the cabin. "It's really lovely here and I could use a day of just relaxing."

"You're welcome, Lina." He gave me another one of those unfamiliar warm smiles and my stomach fluttered with a combination of lust and happiness.

* * *

"Hey, I thought maybe you could use a hot chocolate." I held out the mug of steaming chocolate and Aiden set his hammer down before stripping off his work gloves and taking it from me.

"Thanks." He took a sip as King leaned against my legs. The snow didn't seem to bother the big dog at all and I patted him gently. He licked my mitten-covered hand as I studied Aiden carefully.

Although it was snowing heavily and he had been outside for nearly two hours, he had stripped off his jacket and sweater. I admired the way his muscles flexed under the long-sleeves of his shirt. His cheeks were red from the cold and he looked ridiculously adorable.

"What?" He was watching me stare at him and I could feel a warm blush crossing my cheeks.

"Aren't you cold?" I asked.

He shook his head. "No. Not really."

I glanced at the pile of rotting boards at my feet as Aiden stared at the dark sky. "We're going to have to leave soon. The roads are only going to get worse." He gave me an apologetic look. "Sorry, Lina. It wasn't supposed to storm today."

"That's fine." I hid my disappointment. "

"I'm just going to finish up this last section and then we'll head out. Okay?" Aiden glanced anxiously at the sky again.

"Sounds good. I'll just tidy up the kitchen." I took his mug before wading through the soft snow. It was nearly past my knees and I gave a strangled yelp of surprise when King bounded past me. His large body knocked me flying and I landed face-first in the snow, the mug slipping out of my hand and disappearing in the snow. I struggled to sit up in the deep snow and gave a gasping whoop of relief when Aiden flipped me on to my back.

"Lina, are you okay?" He was squatting next to me and he wiped the snow from my face as I nodded.

"Yes, I'm sorry," I sputtered.

"Sorry for what? It was King who knocked you over." He frowned at me.

"Right," I muttered in embarrassment.

"Here, let me help you up." He reached for my hands and I shook my head.

"I'm fine. I can get up on my own."

"Don't be silly." He scowled at me and took my hands. "I'll help – "

King, barking loudly, came thundering toward us. He barrelled into Aiden, knocking him off his feet and on to me with a harsh thud. I grunted with surprise as his hard body landed on my soft one and started to giggle when King took off, his large paws digging in the snow and showering us in its cold wetness.

Aiden, still lying on top of me, gave me a look of concern. "Lina, I'm sorry! Are you okay?"

I giggled again. "Just ducky, Mr. Wright."

A small smile crossed his face and he pulled his glove off with his teeth before stroking his thumb across my cheek. "You've got snow all over your face again."

I caught my breath at his warm touch and forgot about the coldness seeping into my body. Aiden's gentle touch was enough to set me on fire and when his gaze dropped to my mouth, I bit at my lower lip nervously.

He groaned softly and ran his thumb over my lip. My mouth parted and he groaned again.

"Kiss me. Please, Aiden, I need you," I whispered before I could stop myself. He hesitated, his eyes widening with surprise, and I closed mine in humiliation. These ridiculous fantasies about my boss had to stop. I couldn't be –

I jerked in surprise when his warm lips touched mine. My eyes flew open and my hands clutched at his hard arms as his soft kiss turned unexpectedly rough. I moaned, my fingers digging into his biceps, as he thrust his tongue into my mouth and pressed me deeper into the snow. He kissed me until I was moaning loudly and my pelvis was thrusting against him helplessly.

I had often fantasized about kissing Aiden but the fantasies were nothing compared to the real thing. His kisses were demanding and forceful and I couldn't get enough of them. My body was melting under his touch, surrendering willingly to his demands, and I made a soft cry of protest when he pulled his mouth from mine.

"You taste delicious, Ms. Jones," he muttered thickly.

The sound of a motor broke the silence and King barked joyously and raced toward the snowmobile that was headed toward us. Aiden stood quickly and yanked me to my feet. I brushed the snow from my jacket and pants as the snowmobile stopped next to us and the driver shut off the engine and took off his helmet.

"Hello, Aiden."

"Hi, Joe. How are you?"

"Good." The older man stared curiously at me and I gave him a tentative smile as Aiden cleared his throat.

"Joe Lawson, this is Lina Jones. Lina, this is my good friend, Joe."

Joe grinned at me. "So, this is the infamous Ms. Jones. It's nice to meet you, Lina. Stephanie and I have heard a lot about you."

I blinked in surprise before holding my hand out. "Uh, it's nice to meet you as well, Joe."

I glanced at Aiden. His face was a dull shade of red and he avoided looking at me as Joe patted King. "Hey, big fella."

He glanced up at the sky. "Quite the storm, huh?"

"Yeah. We were just going to pack up and head home before the roads get too bad to drive on," Aiden replied.

"It's too late for that," Joe said cheerily. "Steph sent me over here. We saw you drive in and she was worried that you were going to try and drive home tonight. The storm's only going to get worse and Rudy sent word over the radio that the roads are already slippery as shit."

"Son of a bitch," Aiden said. He gave me an apologetic look. "I'm sorry, Lina. I think we're going to be stuck here tonight."

"Oh, that's okay." I gave him a faint smile. "Better safe than sorry, right?"

"Yes," Aiden sighed and I stared at the snow still clinging to my pants.

If it hadn't been for the weird awkwardness between us, I could have almost believed that the kiss was just another one of my lust-fueled fantasies.

"Why don't you and Lina come for dinner? Steph's making spaghetti and there's plenty for everyone," Joe suggested. "I know she would love to meet Lina."

"Oh, um…" Aiden glanced at me before nodding. "Sure, that sounds great."

"Good!" Joe slid the helmet over his head. "Supper will be ready in an hour or so, but come on by whenever you'd like."

Aiden nodded again as Joe started the snowmobile and drove off.

"I'm sorry, Lina. I should have paid closer attention to how bad the storm was getting," Aiden sighed.

"It's fine," I said with a forced cheerfulness. "I don't mind, really."

"Right." He gave me a look I didn't understand before glancing at the sky again. "Let's go inside and warm up before we leave. Joe and Stephanie don't live far and it'll probably be easiest if we hike over there."

"Okay." I followed him silently into the cabin.

* * *

"Lina! It's so good to meet you!" The short, plump woman pulled me into her embrace before I could even take off my jacket. I returned her hug as she kissed my cheek and grinned at me. "With everything Aiden's told us about you, I feel like I know you already!"

I gave her a bewildered smile before glancing at Aiden. He was steadfastly refusing to look at me, and Stephanie patted King before taking my hand. "Why don't you come into the kitchen with me while the boys relax in the living room?"

I followed her into the kitchen. It smelled delicious and I inhaled deeply as Stephanie stirred a pot full of bubbling sauce. "That smells great, Mrs. Lawson."

"Oh call me Stephanie, please." She smiled at me and nodded to a chair. "Have a seat and we'll chat."

I sat down and smiled at her as she popped a tray of garlic bread into the oven. "You have a lovely home, Stephanie. Do you live here all year around?"

"We do," she replied. "Joe retired a few years ago and we decided to move up here full time. It's so peaceful, I love it."

"It does seem very peaceful," I agreed. "Have you and Joe known Aiden long?"

"Oh a few years now. He spent a lot of time here at the cabin with us and when the old Warren place came up for sale, we weren't surprised when he bought it. He's done wonderful things with that little cabin, hasn't he?"

"It's really nice. I like it a lot," I replied.

"Is this the first time you've been up here?"

I nodded and Stephanie sat her plump body down in the chair next to mine. "I'm surprised by that. I would have thought Aiden would have brought you up here before now."

"Um, I think you might have me mistaken with someone else, Stephanie," I said.

She gave me an odd look. "I don't think so. You work with Aiden, right?"

I nodded again and she smiled at me. "That's what I thought. Aiden is forever going on about what a great assistant you are to him. According to him, you're the best assistant he's ever had."

I blushed and Stephanie giggled like a schoolgirl. "You're a sweet little thing, aren't you? Aiden didn't tell us how pretty you were."

I blushed more deeply before staring at the table. "I'm sure he doesn't think I'm pretty."

Stephanie gave me another odd look. "I'm sure he does. Now, tell me a little bit about yourself, Lina. Aiden hasn't really shared any personal stuff about you with us."

"Well I uh, I grew up in the city. I've worked for about three years for Aiden."

"Lovely. And do you have any siblings?"

"Yes. I have an older sister named Kate."

"Are you close to your parents?"

"Yes."

"Lovely. Has Aiden met them?"

"What?" I blinked at her.

"Has Aiden met your parents?"

I shook my head. "No. Um, Aiden and I just work together. We're not uh, dating or anything like that."

"Oh!" She gave me a look of surprise. "Oh my goodness, I'm so sorry. With the way he talks about you, and then Joe told me that earlier he saw you two…"

She trailed off and gave me a look of embarrassment. "Goodness, I am terribly embarrassed right now."

I smiled at her. "It's fine, Stephanie. You have nothing to be embarrassed about."

She stood and stirred the sauce again. "I do tend to run off at the mouth from time to time."

I laughed. "You and me both."

She grinned at me. "I have a feeling we're going to get along very well, Lina."

Chapter 5

"Now, don't you be a stranger, Lina!" Stephanie stood in the doorway and gave me one last hug. "You're welcome to come to the house anytime you want. You don't have to wait for an invitation. You have my cell number right? I'm going to be in town next week and I'd love to get together for coffee."

"I have it," I confirmed. "Definitely call me and we'll go for coffee. Thank you, Steph. I really enjoyed meeting you and Joe, and thank you again for dinner. It was delicious."

"You're so welcome, sweetie. Aiden – make sure you bring Lina with you the next time you come to the cabin," Stephanie said sternly.

Aiden gave her an uncomfortable smile but didn't say anything as I shook Joe's hand and we left the warmth of their house.

"Toodles! Be careful walking home! Love you!" Stephanie hollered as Joe closed the door.

Aiden and I walked silently through the falling snow. It was very dark and I stumbled a little as King brushed past me and bounded ahead of us. Aiden reached over and took my hand without speaking.

"Thanks."

He nodded and I held his hand tightly as he led me through the deep snow. By the time we reached the cabin, I was feeling the bite of the wind and I hurried into the warmth of the cabin. Aiden dropped my hand and immediately started to build up the fire as I took off my jacket and boots. I perched on one of the stools at the island as Aiden pulled out the couch and gave me an oddly nervous look.

"So, uh, the bedroom is going to be way too cold for you, I think. I'll sleep in there and you can stay out here where it's warmer. The couch is more comfortable than it looks, I swear."

I shook my head immediately. "No, I'll take the bedroom. You said you usually sleep out here in the winter and I don't get cold easily. I'll be fine in the bedroom."

He frowned at me. "You do get cold. You nearly freeze to death in the office for God's sake."

I slid off the stool and walked quickly to the bedroom. "I insist, Aiden. I swear I'll be fine. Good night."

I gave him a large, false smile and disappeared into the bedroom before he could argue again. I leaned against the door and released my breath in a huge rush. Aiden had been quiet and weird the entire night and as much as I had enjoyed Stephanie and Joe's company, his weirdness was freaking me out. He was probably berating himself the entire night for kissing me, and my face burned as I thought back to the way I had begged him to kiss me. Aiden had zero interest in me and I had made a fool of myself with my pathetic begging.

I sighed loudly and quickly stripped out of my jeans and hoodie. I struggled out of my bra, but left my shirt and tank top on. I hesitated before deciding to keep my long underwear and socks on. Shivering, I hurried to the bed and climbed beneath the cold covers. I lay trembling in the middle of the bed, trying to forget the way Aiden's mouth had tasted.

* * *

An hour later I was still wide awake and shaking with cold. I had put my hoodie on again and jammed my toque on my head but the entire bed was vibrating with the force of my shivering. I was just considering hopping out of bed and putting on my jeans when the door opened and Aiden stuck his head in.

"Lina?"

"Yeah?"

"Jesus, it's freezing in here. Get out of bed."

"N-no," I stuttered. "I'm too cold."

"I know. Come on, you need to come into the living room with me. It's warmer in there." He was pulling back the covers and I made a soft whine as the cold air hit me. "Get up, Lina."

Grumbling loudly, I climbed out of bed and watched as he hauled the top mattress, blankets and all, out of the room. I followed him into the living room as he dropped the mattress on the floor. "Get in."

Too cold to argue, I burrowed under the covers and squeaked with surprise when Aiden climbed in behind me.

"What are you doing?"

"Body heat," he said briefly. "We'll both be warmer this way."

I didn't reply as he molded his body to the back of mine. His arm went around my waist and he buried his face between my shoulder blades. "You're freezing."

"I kn-know," I chattered grumpily.

He rubbed my arms roughly. "You'll warm up soon. Try and get some sleep."

"Right," I said. I would never fall asleep with Aiden's hard body plastered up against mine. Of course, I was already feeling warmer and the heat from the fire felt good on my face. I yawned tiredly as my body relaxed and Aiden's arm slipped around my waist again.

"Good night, Lina," he whispered.

"Night," I mumbled.

I woke up a couple of hours later. I had gone from freezing cold to much too warm and I sat up in the bed.

"What's wrong?" Aiden sat up beside me.

"Too hot." I unzipped my hoodie and struggled out of it before yanking my shirt over my head. It left me in just my tank top and I wondered briefly about Aiden's sharp inhale as I pulled the toque off my head and collapsed back on the bed.

I left the covers pooled around my waist, I was so warm I was perspiring, and stretched languidly before yawning.

"Fuck," Aiden muttered.

"What's wrong?" I cracked open one eye and squinted up at him. He wasn't looking at me, his attention was on my breasts and I glanced downward.

"Shit!"

I'd forgotten just how thin and tight my tank top was and without a bra, my breasts were practically busting out of the damn thing.

I reached for the covers, my face a brilliant shade of red, but before I could yank them up, Aiden's hand was circling my wrists and he was pulling my arms above my head.

"What are you doing?" I whispered.

His attention was still solely devoted to my breasts. "You've been teasing me with your delectable tits for the last three years. I think it's time I had a taste, don't you?"

"I haven't been teasing you!" I glared at him as he threw one hard leg over my thighs and pinned me down.

"Haven't you?" He raised his gaze to mine and my panties were instantly wet at the dark lust in his eyes.

"No," I whispered weakly as he used his free hand to pull my tank top upward until it was bunched around my upper chest. He made a growl of approval at the sight of my naked breasts before bending his head and sucking my nipple into his mouth.

I moaned as my nipple hardened into a tight bud and he used his tongue to trace tiny circles around it. When he bit me, my back arched and I cried out with pleasure, my entire body shuddering against his. Part of me believed I was dreaming and I stared wide-eyed at him as he lifted his head and gave me a dark look of desire.

"My little kitten likes that, does she?" Aiden whispered. He took my other nipple into his mouth and teased it with his teeth and tongue until I was writhing and moaning uncontrollably. I pulled frantically at his hand and he tightened it around my wrists before letting go.

I clutched his head in my hands, small whimpers escaping from my mouth, as he pulled and sucked at my throbbing nipples.

"Please, Aiden," I moaned.

"Please what?" He pinched my nipple gently.

"Oh!" I gasped and tugged at his hair. "Please kiss me."

"My pleasure, princess." He kissed me deeply, his tongue sliding in to touch mine and I sucked eagerly on it. This was really happening. My fantasies about him were actually turning into reality and I arched my body against his as we kissed hungrily.

He cupped and kneaded my breasts before tearing his mouth from mine. "You're a responsive little thing, aren't you?"

I blushed and he grinned wickedly and kissed the tip of my nose. "Don't be embarrassed. I like it. Lift your hips."

I raised my hips obediently and he tugged my long underwear down my legs. I kicked them off impatiently, dragging my socks with them, and he pushed me back when I tried to turn on my side to face him.

"No." His voice was firm and a shiver of arousal racked my body. He rested his hand on my stomach and kissed my neck, sucking gently before nipping at my earlobe.

"Open your legs, kitten," he demanded.

I parted them immediately and he made a soft sound of approval before cupping me through my panties. The crotch of them was soaking wet and he grinned again. "So wet already."

"Oh please," I begged.

"Patience, Ms. Jones," he said sternly.

I wiggled my pelvis against his hand before reaching down and cupping him through his track pants. He inhaled sharply, his hips bucking into my hand as I gripped him firmly.

"Naughty girl." He bit my lower lip until I gasped, and then licked away the sting.

I rubbed his cock almost desperately. A part of me was ashamed of my eagerness and obvious need but a larger, stronger part was beyond caring. I had spent the better part of three years lusting after my boss and I wanted him inside of me.

He slid his hand inside my panties and pushed one long finger into my throbbing cunt. I cried out and arched my pelvis as he stared down at me.

"When was the last time you were fucked?" He suddenly asked.

I blinked at him as he slid a second finger into my wet pussy. "W-what?"

"When was the last time you had a cock sliding into this amazingly tight little pussy?" He growled.

"I – I don't know. A long time." I flushed with embarrassment. It had been exactly two years, two months and five days but I wasn't about to tell him that.

"Was it a boyfriend or a random hook up?"

I frowned at him. "What does it matter?"

"Tell me," he insisted. His fingers were still firmly inside of me but he had stopped moving them and I made a small whine of need.

He grinned at the sound. "Tell me what I want to know and I'll move my fingers, kitten."

"Boyfriend," I gasped.

"Why did you break up?"

I sighed with frustration. "We were too different."

"Bullshit," he replied immediately. "People always say they broke up because they were too different. It's rarely the truth."

He pulled his second finger free and I moaned with disappointment. "Aiden, please. You promised."

"Tell me the truth." He used his thumb to rub at my clit and I nearly climaxed all over his hand. He stopped immediately and gave me a look of disapproval.

"You really need to learn control, Ms. Jones."

I panted harshly as my heart thudded heavily in my chest. "Please touch me, Aiden."

"I will." His tone became soothing and he kissed me softly on the mouth. "Now, tell me the truth."

I didn't want to. I had never told anyone, not even my best friend Tracy, the real reason that Kent had broken up with me. The truth was utterly humiliating, but I knew Aiden would leave me aching and needy if I didn't. The thought of not having his cock, of not finding the release I was so desperate for, made me blurt out the truth.

"I – I wasn't good enough in bed for him. He liked lots of different positions and I'm, well I'm heavy and not that flexible, and he was tired of the same old positions. He said if I lost weight and became more adventurous in bed, he would take me back. I didn't lose the weight and he moved on with a thin, pretty girl."

I closed my eyes. The desire had faded from my body and I was left with nothing but the same sick embarrassment I had felt for months after Kent had finally admitted I didn't do it for him in bed. I was a fool if I thought Aiden wouldn't feel the same way the first time he tried to fuck me in something other than the missionary position. I had taken up yoga in the last year, grunting and sweating to a DVD in the privacy of my home, and while I was slightly more flexible than I used to be, I would never be the kind of girl who could put her legs up over her head or get into the intricate sex positions that seemed to be so popular in the porn industry.

"Look at me, Lina."

I shook my head. "No. Can you – can you please let me go? I think it's better if I go back to the bedroom now."

Instead of releasing me, his hand tightened in my hair and he pressed his hard body closer to mine. "No. Look at me, Lina."

I opened my eyes and blinked rapidly, willing myself not to cry. I was already humiliated enough.

Aiden stared down at me. There was anger on his chiseled face and I swallowed nervously.

"Aiden, I – "

"You're beautiful, Lina. Do you hear me? You're absolutely, fucking gorgeous and I'm tempted to find out this asshole's name so I can go to his house and kick his fucking ass for making you think you aren't."

"I – I know I'm pretty," I whispered, "but – "

"Beautiful. You're beautiful. Say it, Lina. Right now," he demanded.

"I'm beautiful," I whispered.

"Fucking beautiful," he growled.

I blushed, heat coursing through me at his words, before I cleared my throat. "He never thought I was ugly, he just wanted someone better in bed which is why I think I should go back to the bedroom."

I hurried on before he could say anything. "Someone like you obviously has a lot of experience, and I – I might have fantasized about having sex with you but fantasies are a lot different than the actual thing."

"What would you say if I told you I was a virgin?" He asked.

My mouth dropped open and I stared blankly at him before giggling. "Like hell you are."

He didn't reply and I bit at my lip. "Oh God. You aren't, are you? I mean, it's fine if you are, I just – "

He suddenly snorted in amusement and I slapped him sharply on the chest. "Asshole!"

He dipped his head, his breath hot in my ear, and sucked on my earlobe for a moment. "I can assure you, Ms. Jones, that I am not a virgin. In fact, I happen to have excellent skills in the bedroom. You'll find out exactly what I mean when you're under me and screaming my name."

"Arrogant asshole," I muttered breathlessly.

He grinned. "Arrogant asshole who's about to fuck you senseless, Ms. Jones."

I moaned as his tongue probed my ear and I clutched at his arms as he slid his finger in and out of my soaking cunt.

"Now, tell me about your fantasies."

"I − what?" I wondered if I could pretend I didn't know what he meant.

"You said you fantasized about me. I want to hear what they are."

"Aiden, no!" I shook my head. "I − it's too embarrassing."

"You will tell me, Ms. Jones, or I'll put you over my knee and spank that delectable bottom of yours until you're begging me to stop."

My pussy clenched around his finger in a glorious, heart-stopping spasm of pleasure and I moaned softly. A wide grin crossed his face and he sucked on my bottom lip, pulling roughly on it.

"Well, well, Ms. Jones. I think I've just discovered one of your fantasies."

I groaned and he gave me a decidedly wicked grin. "Tell me another fantasy. Tell me your favourite one, the one that makes you feel like you're going to come in your panties."

I swallowed thickly and gave him a hesitant look. "It's – it's laundry day and I have nothing to wear but a tight shirt and short skirt."

"Like that day a couple of weeks ago?" He interrupted.

My face went red. "Um, yeah."

"When I walked into my office that evening and saw you bent over my filing cabinet, your ass in its pretty white panties sticking up in the air, it was all I could do not to rip off those panties and stick my cock deep into your pussy. I'd been rock fucking hard all morning watching you parade around in that tight top and short skirt. I had to jerk off in my bathroom at lunch just so I could concentrate on my meetings that afternoon."

I made a soft gasping sound of need and he licked my mouth before whispering, "Go on, Ms. Jones. Tell me the rest of it."

"You call me into your office and tell me that my clothes aren't work appropriate and they've caused a – a large problem," I whispered.

He thrust his finger deeper into my pussy and I shuddered wildly.

"Keep going," he muttered.

"Then you unzip your pants, pull out your cock and tell me to get on my knees and fix the problem."

"Fuck!" He whispered harshly. He used the ball of his thumb to press lightly on my clit and I made a keening noise of pleasure, my fingers digging into his broad back.

"Go on," he said hoarsely.

"I – I get on my knees under your desk and you put your hand on my head and force me to take your cock into my mouth. I suck you and lick you and – "

I moaned, my hips bucking against his hand when he flicked my clit lightly.

"Don't stop," he growled.

"I suck hard and you hold my hair and push more of your cock into my mouth. You're rough but there's a part of me that likes it. I – I want to please you so I try and take as much of you into my mouth as I can."

He pulled his finger from my pussy and rubbed my clit in hard, firm circles. I moaned and whimpered and struggled to form coherent thoughts as pleasure grew in my belly.

"You - you tell me that you're going to come in my mouth and I have to be a good girl and swallow it all."

I was panting harshly now, grinding my pelvis against Aiden's hand, as he licked my collarbone with an agonizingly slow stroke. "And are you a good girl, kitten? Do you swallow all of my cum like a good little princess?"

"Yes!" I cried out as my pussy squeezed uselessly and my orgasm swept through me in a hard, dizzying rush. I collapsed against the mattress, panting loudly and my body trembling. My pussy was still throbbing and clenching. I wanted, *needed*, Aiden's cock inside of me and I didn't protest when he swept my panties down my legs and off my feet.

"Are you on the pill, Lina?"

I opened my eyes and squinted at him in the firelight. He had taken off his t-shirt and I stared hungrily at his chest and abdomen. His abs were clearly defined and I reached out with a shaking hand and curled my fingers into the dark hair on his chest.

His breath hissed out between his teeth and he muttered a curse before ripping my tank top over my head.

"Are you?" He asked again as his hand kneaded my right breast.

"Yes," I moaned.

"I don't have a condom with me."

"Are you kidding me?" I groaned loudly and he pinched my nipple lightly.

"Do *you* have one?"

"No," I sighed. "But I can't believe you don't have one."

"I wasn't intending to seduce my secretary tonight, Ms. Jones," he said dryly.

"Well, fuck." I could feel myself pouting and it must have been apparent because he leaned down and kissed me hard on the mouth.

"God, you're fucking adorable when you pout." He grinned.

I sighed loudly and began to wiggle my hand under the waistband of his track pants. I could at least give him a hand job. It wasn't what I needed, not by a long shot, but I wasn't going to leave him high and dry after he gave me an earth-shattering orgasm.

He caught my hand and pulled it away before kissing the palm of it. "I'm clean, Lina. I get tested regularly and I'm disease free."

I stared at him before whispering, "I am too."

"I want to fuck you, Lina. I won't lie – having you jack me off isn't enough for me. Not after three years of imagining what it would be like to have your tight little pussy clinging to my cock."

I moaned and he stared intently at me. "I promise I'll show you my medical records first thing Monday morning, but if you'd rather not – I won't pressure you. It's your decision, Lina, and I'll respect it."

I studied him for a moment before lifting my head and kissing him hard on the mouth. "I want you to fuck me tonight, Aiden."

"Are you sure?"

I nodded. "Yes, I trust you. And I'll show you my records on Monday too."

A large smile crossed his face and I inhaled sharply when he abruptly shoved his track pants down his legs. I stared at his large cock. The head was a slightly darker shade than the shaft and he was thick and long.

His hand threaded through my long hair and gripped tightly. "Your mouth first, princess. You're going to suck my cock until I tell you to stop."

I leaned over him eagerly and slid my mouth down over the head of his cock. He groaned loudly and fresh lust flooded through me. He gathered my hair into a pony tail and tugged sharply when I closed my eyes.

"Keep your eyes open and look up at me," he demanded.

I stared up at him obediently as I licked and sucked on his cock. He traced my lips with the head of his cock and I licked away the precum, moaning a little at the intoxicating taste of him.

"That's my good girl," he said hoarsely. "Suck harder."

I tightened my lips around his cock and sucked firmly. He thrust his hips into my mouth and groaned again before holding my head firmly in his hands and plunging his cock in and out. I opened my mouth wide and let him control the pace, watching his face as he panted and moaned.

"Christ, Lina," he muttered harshly before giving me a naughty grin. "I'm starting to think I need to add this to your list of job duties."

I traced the head of his cock with my tongue and he moaned again. "Would you like that, kitten? Would you like to start every day on your knees with your hot mouth stuffed full of my cock?"

I nodded and stroked the base of his cock with my hand before sucking aggressively.

He stiffened and quickly pulled me off his cock before pushing me roughly on to my back. "Fuck! You're going to make me come, princess."

I stared up at him. I had never been much for nicknames, tolerating the 'babe' and 'sugar' that Kent would occasionally call me but it was different with Aiden. Hearing him call me 'princess' and 'kitten', in that deep, slightly sarcastic tone did strange things to my insides and only added to my deep desire.

"Spread your legs."

I parted them eagerly and rubbed myself against him when he settled his body between my thighs. He kissed me hard on the mouth before reaching between us and guiding his cock into my pussy. I cried out and thrust my hips upwards. He groaned loudly as I squeezed my inner muscles around his thick cock.

"Jesus, you're killing me," he muttered. "Your pussy is so fucking tight, kitten."

I bucked my pelvis against his, wrapping my arms around his waist and clinging tightly to him as I took his cock deep inside of me.

He cursed again. "Stop, Ms. Jones. You're much too impatient."

"No!" I bit his broad shoulder in near desperation. "I need you, Aiden."

A small smile crossed his face and he grabbed my wrists and yanked them above my head, pinning them to the mattress before using his large body to stop the motion of my hips against him. I whined in protest and he licked my mouth quickly.

"My kitten needs to be fucked hard and rough. Is that it?"

"Yes!" I moaned. "Yes!"

"Whatever you need, princess," he whispered.

He rose to his knees and, still holding my wrists captive with one hand, thrust into me with hard, deep strokes. His other hand tugged and rubbed at my hard nipples as he drove in and out of my wet pussy.

I had never been so wet in my life and I should have been embarrassed by the loud, sucking sounds my pussy made as it clung eagerly to his cock. I wasn't. Hell, I wasn't even embarrassed by the mewls of need and begging that was spilling from my lips. My legs were stretched so widely around his large body that my thigh muscles were burning but the slight pain was buried beneath a wave of pleasure as Aiden pounded my body into the mattress in a steady, relentless rhythm.

I closed my eyes and concentrated. Aiden was thicker than Kent and I could feel him rubbing snugly against the walls of my pussy. It was a different sensation, one that sent large shivers of pleasure up and down my spine, and I concentrated on that feeling, trying to will myself into an orgasm.

Aiden's rhythm was changing, turning into long, slow strokes instead of hard and fast and I moaned softly as he kissed me hungrily.

"Can you come from being fucked, Lina?" He suddenly whispered.

My eyes popped open in a hurry and I gave him a wary look, my body tensing under his. Had he somehow read my damn mind?

He released my hands and nibbled lightly on my bottom lip as his hips continued their unhurried rhythm. "Can you?"

I eyed him carefully, trying to read the look in his eyes, as I considered what to say. Although I loved sex, loved the feel of a cock sliding into my pussy, I had never had an orgasm from sex alone. I knew there were other women who could, a fact that Kent had often threw in my face, but I'd never been able to. It had frustrated Kent to the point of anger and after listening to him rant about my, as he put it, 'dysfunctional pussy', I had finally started faking orgasms.

I had confessed to Tracy and she had rolled her eyes and shook her head in disgust.

"Men and their dicks," she had scoffed. "They get so worked up over their little joysticks. God forbid if a woman can't have an orgasm from the thrusting alone of their all mighty cock. Jesus, Lina, don't listen to anything that dickwad says about sex. If he was a real man, he'd find creative ways to make you orgasm rather than berate you for not being able to come from his little, jabbing dick stick. When are you going to dump that goddamn loser?"

"Lina?" Aiden prompted. He was giving me a serious look and he had stopped moving. For a moment I was tempted to tell him the truth but Tracy was right – men didn't like the idea that a woman couldn't orgasm from their cocks alone – and the thought of disappointing Aiden worried me. After nearly three years with Kent I was an expert at faking orgasms, Aiden would never know.

I gave him what I hoped was a seductive smile and cooed lightly, "Of course. Why are you stopping? I was so close."

I lifted my head and licked his neck with my warm tongue before pushing my hips against him. "Keep going. Please."

His hand gripped the back of my neck and he pulled my head back, his fingers tangling tightly in my hair as he stared at me. "I don't like it when you lie to me, Lina."

"I'm not lying," I whispered.

He studied me carefully and I breathed a sigh of relief when he started to move again. His hand cupped my breast and I arched my back before closing my eyes.

"Oh," I moaned loudly. "That feels so good, Aiden. I'm so close, I'm so – "

I gripped his arms, digging my nails into his biceps as I arched my back, and made a loud, drawn out cry of pleasure. I squeezed him tightly with my pussy and shivered wildly before collapsing against the mattress.

"So good," I moaned again.

When there was no reply, I opened my eyes and stared up at Aiden.

"That was quite the performance, princess," he said dryly.

My face burned dully. "I'm sorry. I can't orgasm this way. It's not your fault though, it's all me. Please don't stop. It feels really good. I just – I'm not normal but I like the way it feels and I don't want you to stop fucking me, okay?"

"Christ," he said, "I swear I really am going to find that fucking asshole and beat the shit out of him."

"I'm sorry," I whispered.

"You have nothing to be sorry about." He was still hard and throbbing within me but I was mesmerized by the look of anger in his eyes.

"I don't ever want you faking an orgasm with me again. Do you understand, Lina?"

"Yes," I whispered again.

"I don't care how you come, only that you come. Is that clear?"

I nodded and he brushed his lips against mine. "I'll spank you for every orgasm you fake, princess."

My pussy clenched helplessly around him at the thought and he made a harsh groan before grinning at me. "Fuck, I'm tempted to spank you right now."

"Aiden," I moaned.

"Next time," he said and propped himself above me on his hands before beginning a smooth slide and retreat motion.

It really did feel amazing and I moaned encouragingly as I clutched at his waist. He took my right hand and guided it between us.

"Touch yourself," he whispered. "I don't want to see you move your hand from that sweet, wet pussy of yours until you actually come. Understand?"

I nodded and slid my fingers between my wet lips and rubbed eagerly at my swollen, slippery clit. I moaned loudly as pleasure exploded in my belly and stroked my clit harder and faster. I pulled lightly on it and jerked against Aiden as I nearly came.

"Oh God!" I groaned as I resumed circling my clit with the tips of my fingers. "I'm going to come, Aiden. I can't – I can't..."

"Don't hold back, Lina," he panted. He was driving into me now, sweat dripping down his chest as the light from the fire danced across his face. "I want to feel you come while I'm fucking you."

I cried out at his words, arching my back as my nipples tightened into hard buds and my climax roared through me like a freight train. I shook wildly under him, one hand digging into his waist and the other rubbing furiously at my clit, as he thrust deeply. He tried to retreat and my pussy clamped down around him like a vise, holding him firmly inside of me.

"Fuck!" He shouted harshly, his back arching and the cords standing out in his neck as he climaxed. I could feel him pulsing inside of me and warmth coated my insides as my pussy eagerly milked his cock for every last drop.

He shouted again, his entire body shaking, before he collapsed against my soft body. I rubbed his slick back, feeling the muscles trembling under my touch, and kissed the side of his neck. He twitched and then slid from my body to his side of the bed.

"Holy shit," he muttered before turning and rolling me to my side. He drew up the covers and spooned me snugly, cupping my large breast and kissing the back of my shoulder before resting his head on the pillow next to mine.

"Go to sleep, Lina," he commanded softly.

Barely able to keep my eyelids open, I pushed my ass more firmly into him and nodded. "Night, Aiden."

"Good night, Lina."

Chapter 6

"Wake up, Ms. Jones." A hard hand shook me from my slumber and I sat up, clutching the covers to my naked chest and blinking blearily at Aiden.

"What? What's wrong?"

"Nothing. But we should get going. It's stopped snowing and Joe has already plowed the driveway and enough of the side road to get us back to the main road. It's not snowing now but it's supposed to start up again and unless you want to be trapped here for another night, I suggest you get dressed quickly."

I nodded and pushed my hair back from my face. "What time is it?"

"Just after eight." He stood and walked outside, letting in a blast of cold air and a bright ray of sunlight, before slamming the door behind him.

There was a soft woof and then King was enthusiastically licking my face. I pushed him away gently before scratching his massive chest.

"At least you still like me this morning," I sighed before grabbing my clothes and scurrying naked to the bathroom.

* * *

I stared blankly out the window of the SUV. We were nearly to my house and the car was so thick with tension that I felt physically ill from it. Aiden had withdrawn completely and I could hardly breathe from the feelings of regret and shame. What had I been thinking? That I would wake up this morning and Aiden would be exactly like he was last night? I wasn't good in bed, I knew I wasn't, but I had still gone ahead and fucked him because I was a desperate and horny pathetic mess. Aiden had temporarily lost his mind last night or else he'd been just horny enough to fuck whoever was willing to part her legs for him, no matter how much she sucked in the sack.

"Lina, we need to talk," Aiden said quietly.

I groaned to myself. We were pulling into my driveway and I had actually hoped that I could just say my goodbye and get the hell out of Dodge.

"Ok." I continued to stare out the window as he put the vehicle in park.

"What happened last night was a mistake. You're my employee and I should have never engaged in sexual activities with you."

I winced at the coldness of his description before nodding. "Yes, you're right."

"It's not just that I'm your boss," he continued. "I'm not interested in a relationship and you don't strike me as the type of woman who would be happy with an occasional roll in the hay."

"You're right," I said again.

He sighed. "Lina, look at me, please."

Steeling myself, I turned to face him. "I know it was a mistake and I'm not going to – to freak out or start stalking you or anything like that. And I'm not going to quit my job again, at least not over this. Your inability to not be an asshat, however..."

He didn't smile at my small joke and I sighed in defeat. "It's fine, Mr. Wright. I understand, really."

"I'm sorry, Lina. I'm being a real shithead, I know, but I think it's better if you hear the truth. Obviously I'm attracted to you, have been for three years, and I got caught up in the moment. I feel terrible that I did this to you. I don't do relationships, and I certainly don't do relationships with my employees."

"Fair enough. Thanks for being honest with me." I reached for the door handle, stiffening when he reached out and caught my arm.

"What's happening right now has nothing to do with the actual sex. You know that, right? The sex was amazing and I enjoyed it very much."

"I know," I lied brightly. "I should get going. I'll see you tomorrow, Mr. Wright."

"Lina, I mean it. You're not awful in bed like your asshole of an ex-boyfriend tried to convince you that you were."

I shrugged carelessly. "You shared my bed for one night - he shared it for nearly four years. I think he's probably better qualified to make that call."

"Lina," he gave me an exasperated look, "this has nothing to do with your abilities in bed. I don't – "

"It's fine." I tugged my arm free. "It's not that big of a deal anyway. We're going back to the way things were, remember?"

He sighed in frustration but I had already opened the door and slid out. "Good bye, Mr. Wright. Thanks for the weekend away – it was uh, really nice. I'll see you at the office tomorrow."

I shut the door before he could reply and scurried into my house. I slammed the door behind me and leaned against it as the hot tears leaked down my face. My humiliation was like a living, pulsing thing inside me and I covered my face with my hands. I knew, despite what Aiden had tried to say otherwise, that my chubby body, my inability to even orgasm without it being a whole goddamn production, and my pathetic sex skills in general were the real reasons for his rejection. I wanted nothing more than to curl up into my bed and never leave it but I already looked like a pathetic mess to Aiden. I would scoop up the little bit of pride I had left and do my job like a goddamn professional.

* * *

"Excuse me?"

I looked up from my computer screen and gave the tall, blond man standing in front of me a friendly smile. "Hello."

"Hi, my name is Jamie Parker, I'm the new – "

"CFO," I finished. "It's nice to meet you, Mr. Parker."

He gave me a surprised look. "How did you know that?"

I laughed. "I'm Mr. Wright's assistant. It's my job to know everything that's happening in the office."

He grinned and leaned one narrow hip against my desk before folding his arms across his broad chest. He glanced quickly at my breasts before giving me another easy grin. "Impressive. Tell me Ms. - "

"Jones. Lina Jones."

"Lina. You have a beautiful name, Lina."

"Thank you." I could feel a smile crossing my face as he held out his hand and I shook it firmly.

"So tell me, Lina, what else do you know about me?"

"Let's see," I ticked off each point on my fingers, "you come to us from a large public accounting firm. You were the youngest person in the history of the company to make partner, you're an avid skier and you play guitar."

He gave me an admiring look. "Impressive. How did you know all of that?"

I shrugged. "Mr. Wright had me do some research before we hired you. It wasn't hard to find the article about you donating your time to helping disabled children learn to ski."

"And the guitar playing?"

I pointed to his left hand. "Calluses on the tips of your fingers. Dead giveaway."

He laughed loudly. "Very clever, Lina."

"Thank you." I gave him a modest smile and he laughed again before leaning closer.

"So, does this mean I need to come to you for the office dirt?"

I shook my head. "Nope. I never reveal office secrets, Mr. Parker."

"Call me Jamie."

"Jamie." I smiled at him before standing and smoothing down my skirt. "I know you have an appointment with Mr. Wright but he's just finishing up a phone call. Can I grab you a cup of coffee?"

He shook his head. "I'm perfectly capable of getting my own cup of coffee."

"I don't mind. I usually get Mr. Wright's coffee for him."

"Really? You know, the guy doesn't look seventy years old."

I snorted soft laughter as I picked up my coffee mug and Mr. Wright's. "Don't let him hear you say that."

He followed me down the hallway and into the kitchen. "Yeah, I've heard all about his reputation. Seeing how he has such a sweet, tender-hearted assistant though, I'm starting to wonder if he isn't all bark and no bite."

I laughed again as I poured coffee into my mug. "Now, what makes you think I'm sweet, Mr. Parker? You barely know me."

He gave me a careless grin. "Let's just say I'm good at reading people."

"Really?"

"Yes, in fact I can tell exactly what you're thinking right now."

"That's quite the skill. Why are you wasting your time crunching numbers?" I poured coffee into Mr. Wright's mug before reaching into the fridge for the cream.

When I turned around Jamie had moved behind me and was leaning against the counter. "Reading people's minds doesn't pay nearly as well as crunching numbers."

"Not surprising," I replied. "So, what am I thinking right now?"

He cocked his head at me. "You're wondering if during all of your research on me if you just missed the information about a girlfriend, or if someone this good looking and charming really could be single."

"Wow. You are good," I said mockingly.

He laughed. "It's a gift. Let me save you some research time and assure you that I am most definitely single."

"Congratulations," I said cheerfully.

"And you? Are you single, Lina?"

"Couldn't be more single if I tried."

He grinned and stepped closer until I could feel his warm breath on my face. His eyes were hazel with flecks of green in them and his face was shaved smooth.

"There's an eyelash on your cheek." He swiped his thumb lightly across my cheek bone before showing me the dark lash on it. "Make a wish."

I smiled and closed my eyes before blowing lightly on his thumb. When I opened my eyes, Jamie was staring at my mouth and I licked my lips nervously.

Jamie cleared his throat. "Lina, would you like to go – "

"Ms. Jones!"

I jerked, teetered on my heels and would have fallen if Jamie hadn't grabbed my arm.

"Okay?" He asked.

"Yes, thank you. " I turned to Aiden.

"Yes, Mr. Wright?"

"I'm supposed to be meeting with Mr. Parker." He was staring at us like an angry bull and I smiled politely at him.

"I realize that. I was getting your coffee for the meeting." I reached for his cup and handed it to him as he glared at Jamie.

"Mr. Parker, my office now."

He turned and stalked out of the kitchen as Jamie gave me a thoughtful look. "Something has him all riled up."

"Something always does," I said cheerfully. "Have a good meeting."

"Thanks." He grinned and left the kitchen.

The smile dropped my face and I leaned against the counter. My heart was pounding and I wiped a hand across my face.

It had been a month since the cabin. Monday morning Aiden had emailed me his medical records. I had emailed mine in return without saying anything and that was the last mention of our night at the cabin. Although Aiden was true to his word and actually treated me better than before I quit, it was still a struggle to come to work every day. He was perfectly polite, most of the time, but there was a tension between us that never went away. I sighed miserably and picked up my cup of coffee. Despite his rejection, I still wanted him desperately. I wished bitterly for the hundredth time that I had never gone to the cabin with him. It was worse now, knowing exactly what it was like to have him between my legs, and I couldn't seem to get over my need for him.

I was an idiot. I had obviously made a terrible impression in the sack and yet, I couldn't stop hoping that Aiden still wanted me. He didn't. He was completely over me and I swallowed down my disappointment and self-pity and returned to my desk. If I didn't get over this soon, I would find another job. The raise and Aiden's better treatment wasn't worth going insane.

* * *

"Well, fancy meeting you here." Jamie dropped into the chair across from me.

I smiled at him. "Mr. Parker. Survived your meeting with Mr. Wright, did you?"

"Just barely." He laughed before scanning the menu board of the small café we were sitting in. "What's good here?"

"The mushroom soup is delicious." I took another sip of soup as Jamie watched.

"I had a very interesting discussion with Mr. Wright at our meeting this morning," he said.

"Oh?" I feigned disinterest as I bit into my piece of garlic toast.

"Yes. We talked about you, actually."

"Odd," I replied neutrally.

"Are you and Mr. Wright dating?"

I choked on my toast and coughed raggedly as Jamie reached across and pounded me on the back.

"You okay?"

"Yes," I croaked out before taking a sip of water. "Why would you ask me that?"

"Because Mr. Wright told me you were off limits."

I blinked at him. "He what?"

"He said you were off limits. Those were his exact words."

I frowned. "Why would he say that?"

"You tell me."

"I have no idea. We're not dating." I pushed away my bowl of soup and tried to keep from blushing as Jamie stared thoughtfully at me.

"I didn't think so, but thought I would ask. I asked him if you two were fucking."

This time I choked on my water and Jamie patted me again on the back. "Sorry, that was coarse of me. I meant to say that I asked him if you two were making the beast with two backs."

I snorted laughter. "Oh, that's much better, Jamie."

He winked at me. "He denied it."

"Of course he did." I gave him a look of fake indignation. "I'm not the kind of employee who sleeps with her boss."

"I didn't see anything in the employee handbook about coworkers not being allowed to date," he said casually.

"There isn't but that doesn't mean I'm going to hump my boss," I replied.

He laughed. "Fair enough. But you know he wants to fuck you, right?"

"Jamie!" I glanced around nervously. Several of our coworkers were in the café and I glared at him. "Keep your voice down."

He leaned closer. "Sorry. I'm just trying to figure out the situation here. Good old Mr. Wright wants to fu – sorry, make sweet, sweet love – to his assistant, that much is obvious, and I'm wondering if his assistant feels the same way."

"Why do you care?" I asked.

He grinned. "Do I have to spell it out for you, Lina?"

I blushed and looked down at the table. "You don't even know me."

"I'd like to get to know you but not if my boss is going to take me behind the building and beat the shit out of me for hitting on his woman."

"One – I'm not his woman and two – he doesn't want to sleep with me. He doesn't like the idea of coworkers dating, that's all."

"Sure, that's all it is." He reached out and traced my knuckles with the tip of his finger. "So, what do you say, Lina? Would you like to go out?"

I hesitated. Jamie was handsome and funny and I was tempted to say yes. If only to figure out why on earth he would be interested in my chubby body and average looks.

"I – can I think about it?"

"Of course." He jumped up and started toward the counter. "Do you mind if I have lunch with you?"

I shook my head and he grinned like a schoolboy. "Great. It's our first date."

I rolled my eyes, giggling a little despite myself, and watched as he walked confidently to the counter.

Chapter 7

"Merry Christmas, Lina!" Amanda threw her arms around me and kissed me wetly on the cheek before giggling.

I grinned and returned her hug. "Are you drunk, Amanda?"

"I'm not *not* drunk," she giggled again.

"Tell me you're not driving."

"Of course I'm not. Tell me why you're not drinking." She eyed my glass of water before taking another sip of wine.

"Because I'm driving."

"Oh please." She rolled her eyes. "You know as well as I do that Mr. Wright has taxi chits for everyone. Hell, you were the one handing them out earlier. C'mon, girl, relax and have a glass of wine, enjoy yourself. You're about to have eight whole days of freedom."

She glanced around the lobby of our office building. "Mr. Wright might be a bastard, but the man knows how to throw a party."

I followed her gaze. Nearly everyone in the office was milling around, chatting and drinking wine and eating appetizers. It was the last day before we closed for the holidays and I had spent the last four days preparing for an impromptu office gathering. I had been stressed out until the last minute with calls to caterers, decorators and trying to find a band that would play on short notice."

"Yes, he does," I said dryly.

Amanda grinned. "I guess I should say that you know how to throw a party. You did a great job, Lina."

"Thank you, Amanda," I said as a server drifted toward us. He was carrying a tray filled with glasses of wine and Amanda scooped one from his tray before snatching my glass of water and placing it on the tray.

"Here. Drink this," she ordered.

I sipped at the wine. It wouldn't hurt to have just one. I deserved the damn thing.

"So, are you hitting that or what?" Amanda asked conversationally.

"What?"

She raised her chin in Jamie's direction. He was talking animatedly to the director of marketing and I shook my head.

"No, I'm not hitting that."

"You should be," Amanda replied. "The man has it bad for you."

"It's not good to sleep with your coworkers."

"Oh, pul-leease." She rolled her eyes. "Coworkers hook up all the time now, girl. There's not nearly the stigma there used to be about it."

I sighed. "It's just asking for trouble, Amanda."

She laughed. "You could use a little trouble in your life, Lina. You're way too well-behaved and sweet for your own good. I thought maybe you had changed when you screamed at Mr. Wright, flipped him the bird and quit on the spot, but then you came back."

"Not that I'm not glad you're back but I don't know if I ever told you how badass that was," she added hastily.

I laughed. "It wasn't badass."

"Fuck, yes it was!" She insisted. "The office gossip mill was talking for days about how you ripped Mr. Wright a new one and he went to your house begging you to come back to work for him. People were actually starting to think he had feelings. Until he fired poor Cynthia a week later."

"Cynthia was smoking weed in the bathroom!" I replied. "Of course he was going to fire her."

"Yeah, but he did it in a spectacular fashion. You have to admit it. I've never seen a grown woman cry so hard in my life."

I didn't reply and Amanda nudged me lightly. "Seriously, Lina. You should go out with Jamie. He's got a bit of a reputation as a playboy but personally, I think that's exactly what you need. Get out there and have some fun, for fuck's sake."

"I'll think about it," I said quickly before changing the subject. "When do you leave for Hawaii?"

"Day after tomorrow. Just me and Kathleen for seven glorious days. I tell you, we're going to make this our new Christmas tradition. No listening to her grandmother tell us we're going to burn in hell, no listening to my Uncle Jack try and convince us that all we need is the right man to turn us straight. It's just me and my smoking hot woman in a bikini, lying on a beach."

I grinned. "It sounds like fun."

"What about you? Your folks coming out?"

I shook my head. "No. They're going to my sister Kate's house this year. I was going to join them but it's an expensive trip. I'm going to fly out after the holidays when there are some deals on flights. Besides, I just know Mr. Wright is going to ask me to come in at some point during the holidays. He always does."

Amanda rolled her eyes. "He's such a Grinch. You're not spending Christmas alone, are you?"

"No. I have a friend who owns a cabin. I'm going up Christmas Eve and will spend a few days with her and her family."

"Nice." Amanda took another sip of her wine. "You could always ask Jamie if he wanted to spend some time with you. I bet he'd jump at the chance."

"Give it a rest, Amanda," I advised lightly.

She shrugged. "I just want you to have some fun, that's all." She lowered her voice as Jamie started toward us. "Speak of the devil."

"Hello, ladies. Enjoying the party?" Jamie smiled cheerfully at us.

"You know it. Although not as much as some of us are." Amanda laughed.

"Oh good grief," I said.

Peter and Lisa were bumping and grinding against each other in front of the band as a few of our co-workers cheered them on. As we watched, Peter grabbed Lisa, dipped her dramatically and kissed her passionately.

"Isn't Lisa married?" I asked.

Amanda shook her head. "Nah, her and Cliff separated two months ago."

Peter's hand drifted to Lisa's ass and squeezed firmly and my eyes widened. "I had no idea Peter was like this. He's always so quiet."

Jamie snickered. "He's an accountant. We're naughty, baby."

I laughed as Amanda tipped her glass toward us. "Well, I'll just leave you two alone to get better acquainted, shall I?"

She gave us an exaggerated wink and I flushed lightly as Jamie chuckled before taking a drink of his beer.

"You've been avoiding me, Ms. Jones."

"I haven't," I protested. "I've been working my ass off to get this damn party ready in time."

"Well, you've done a lovely job." He raised his beer bottle and I clinked it lightly with my wine glass.

"To Ms. Jones. The best party planner in the business."

"Thank you, Mr. Parker." I took a sip of wine as loud cheering came from the direction of the band.

"Oh good Lord," I groaned. Peter was stripping off his jacket and unbuttoning the first few buttons of his shirt. As we watched, he dropped to the floor and began to break dance to the delight of our coworkers.

Jamie took my arm. "Come on, let's go somewhere a little quieter."

He led me to the far end of the lobby. There was no one near us and I admired the twinkling lights that were strung along the wall as Jamie stroked my arm lightly.

"Are you around for the holidays?" He asked. "I thought maybe we could get together for drinks."

"Actually, I'll be out of town." I gave him an apologetic smile.

"That's too bad." He glanced up and then gave me an innocent look. "Well, looks like we're caught under the mistletoe."

I stared up at the small plant twisted around one of the light fixtures before giving him a suspicious look. "Did you move me here on purpose?"

He grinned. "Guilty as charged, Ms. Jones."

He put his arm around my waist and drew me up against his hard body. "I know you're dying to find out what it's like to kiss this handsome devil."

A small smile crossed my face and I closed my eyes and puckered my lips in an exaggerated pout.

"Nice." He laughed before placing a soft kiss on my lips.

I opened my eyes and grinned at him. "Merry Christmas, Jamie."

He kissed me again, this time with an open mouth, and I didn't protest when he slipped his tongue between my lips and stroked my tongue. It was a warm and soft kiss and he tightened his arm around my waist and pulled me closer.

As we kissed I couldn't help comparing his gentle coaxing kiss to the rough, demanding ones of Aiden. I preferred Aiden's, I thought dimly as Jamie deepened the kiss. I craved the way he took my mouth like it was his every right, like he knew exactly how badly I needed him and what he would –

"Ms. Jones!"

As if my very thoughts had summoned him, Aiden's deep voice spoke almost in my ear. I pulled away from Jamie and gave Aiden a guilty look as Jamie scowled.

"Can we help you, Aiden?"

"I require Ms. Jones' help with a work-related issue."

"It's after work," Jamie said. "Is it really necessary to drag her away from the party?"

Aiden sighed loudly. "She's my assistant, Mr. Parker."

"That's right – your assistant. She's not your personal slave. You can't just – "

I took one look at Aiden's rapidly-reddening face and pressed my hand into Jamie's arm. "It's fine. I don't mind at all," I said quickly.

"Lina, you don't have – "

I squeezed Jamie's arm as he continued to protest.

"It's not a problem." I smiled at him. "I won't be long, okay?"

He nodded and I followed Aiden to the elevator.

We rode the elevator in complete silence. I was still holding my glass of wine and I drained it quickly as Aiden stared straight ahead. The doors opened and I followed him down the hall and into his office. I set my empty wine glass on his desk as he slammed the door shut and stalked toward me.

"What do you need help with, Mr. Wright?" I asked quietly.

"Are you fucking Parker?" He barked at me.

I blinked in surprise and took a step back. "What?"

He moved closer. "Are you fucking Parker?" He gritted out.

"That's none of your business!" I snapped at him.

He yanked me into his embrace. My long hair was in a ponytail and he wrapped his hand in it and pulled my head back until my face was pointed toward him.

"You will tell me what I want to know, princess," he growled.

"I will not!" I glared at him. "My personal life is none of your goddamn business, Mr. Wright, and I – "

He kissed me hard on the mouth, thrusting his tongue between my lips and overpowering me with his scent and his touch. I moaned, melting against him, as he took my mouth in a hard, punishing kiss. This was what I wanted, what I had been craving for weeks, and I returned his kiss almost angrily.

We broke apart, both of us breathing raggedly, and I moaned again when I felt his erection pressing against my stomach. He was resting his forehead against mine and I took a deep breath before pulling away and turning around. I stared down at his desk, my thoughts in turmoil and my lust raging out of control.

"This is a mistake," I said hoarsely. "You know it is."

He grunted harshly in frustration before pressing his body against mine. He ground his cock against my ass and reached around to cup my large breasts through my top. He kneaded them roughly before raking my top down my arm and biting me firmly in the spot where my neck became my shoulder. I cried out, my back arching, and he bit me again before his fingers reached for the buttons on my shirt.

"Mr. Wright – "

"Has he done this to you, Lina? Has he touched what belongs to me?"

He yanked my shirt down my arms and clawed open the front clasp of my bra, freeing my breasts from its tight grip. He dropped my bra to the floor before cupping my breasts. He pinched my nipples, pulling roughly on them as I pressed my ass against his cock.

"Has he fucked what is mine and only mine to fuck?" He snarled into my ear.

"No," I moaned breathlessly. I couldn't think past my overwhelming need and my skin felt like it was on fire as Aiden reached for the hem of my skirt. He pulled it up around my waist and I cried out when he pushed his hand into my tights and panties and cupped my throbbing pussy.

"This is mine. Understand?" He growled.

I nodded and didn't protest when he pushed me face down on to his desk. He shoved my tights down to my ankles and pushed my legs apart with his foot. I squeaked in alarm when he tore off my panties and stuffed them into his jacket pocket.

"Wider," he snarled again. "Spread them wider, princess."

I spread my legs further apart, feeling the cool air on my bare ass as he unzipped his pants. I moaned with pleasure when he slammed his cock deep into my wet pussy, my back arching and my ass thrusting back against him.

He pressed his hand in the small of my back, holding me against his desk, as he thrust in and out. His right hand moved from my back to cover my mouth just as his left hand slapped me hard on the ass. His hand muffled my loud squeal of surprise and he spanked me again as I jerked against his desk. The wood was smooth and cool against my naked breasts and I squirmed against it in protest when he spanked me a third time.

"You're being spanked because you let that asshole Parker kiss you. Do you understand?" He whispered harshly.

I nodded and squirmed again when his hand connected with a hard thwack against my naked flesh. He moaned loudly, the sound making me wiggle with pleasure, before leaning over me.

"Every time I spank you, your pussy squeezes my cock so fucking hard," he muttered. "I can barely stop from coming."

I moaned in response as he kissed me again. "Do you like it when I spank you, kitten?"

"Yes!" I gasped. "Yes, I like it!"

"Good girl," he whispered. He kissed me hard before straightening and caressing my burning ass with his big, warm hand. "Your ass looks so pretty with my handprints on it."

"Oh please, Aiden," I begged.

He reached between my legs and rubbed my clit firmly as he fucked me hard and rough. I cried out and he slapped my pussy lightly, sending a bolt of pleasure down my legs.

"Quiet, princess," he ordered. "Do you want the entire office to know I'm fucking you on my desk?"

"Please!" I begged again.

He thrust back and forth roughly but kept his fingers still against my clit. "I have spent the last month dreaming about your soft voice begging, about your tight pussy and how good it feels around my cock," he muttered.

"Aiden, I – "

"You're driving me insane, Lina," he whispered.

He slammed his cock deep into my pussy and pinched my clit roughly. I threw my arm over my mouth and screamed into it as every nerve ending exploded in pleasure. Faintly I was aware of his own hoarse groan as he pumped furiously into me and warmth flooded through me. I panted harshly, resting my cheek against the cool wood of his desk as he rested his forehead against my naked back and rubbed my ass soothingly.

"Are you okay, Lina?" He asked quietly.

I shook my head and struggled to stand. He pulled out of me and I straightened and quickly pulled up my tights before yanking down my skirt.

"Are you hurt?" He asked me worriedly. "I'm sorry. I was too rough. I shouldn't have – "

"I'm not hurt," I interrupted. I reached for my bra and, my face red, struggled into it as he zipped up his pants and picked up my shirt from the floor.

I snatched it from him and he touched my arm gently. "Lina – "

"No." I shook my head. "This was a mistake. You know it was, Aiden."

He sighed. "Lina – "

I buttoned my top and shook my head again. "This shouldn't have happened. I have a – a chance for a real relationship with a perfectly nice, perfectly normal, man and I'm ruining it by fucking you in your goddamn office."

"Parker is not a nice guy," he snapped. "He's a player, Lina."

"And you're not?" I snapped back. "You told me yourself you weren't interested in anything more than fucking."

"That's different."

I laughed bitterly. "How exactly is it different, Mr. Wright?"

"It's different because I – "

He hesitated and I wiped angrily at the tears that were starting to drip down my cheeks. "Can we just forget this happened? Please. I – I don't want to quit my job but I can't stand this torment."

He swallowed heavily. "Please don't quit, Lina. I won't touch you again. I promise."

I nodded and held my hand out. "My panties. Give them back to me."

"They're ripped."

"Fuck! Great – now I have to go back to the goddamn work Christmas party and parade around my coworkers without underwear." I yanked my hairband out of my hair and quickly smoothed my hair before pulling it into a ponytail again.

"I have to go."

"Don't go, Lina. We need to talk. I don't want you to quit because of what I've done. I'm not – "

I held my hand up. "I'm not quitting, Aiden, but I told Jamie I wouldn't be very long. He's going to come looking for me if I don't get back downstairs."

I headed for the door and paused when he called my name.

"What?"

"I — have a good Christmas, Ms. Jones," he said quietly.

"You as well, Mr. Wright," I replied and slipped out of his office.

Chapter 8

I knocked on the door of the cabin and shifted my suitcase in my hand. The door opened and Stephanie beamed at me.

"Lina! I'm so glad you're here. Come in out of the cold." She ushered me in and I set my suitcase down as she took my coat and hung it on a hook on the wall.

"It's so good to – "

She paused and gave me a long look. "Honey, you look terrible."

I laughed. "Thanks, Stephanie."

She pressed her hand to my forehead. "Are you sick, honey?"

"No. Just tired and it's been uh, a bit rough at work lately."

She hugged me gently. "Is that Aiden of ours giving you a hard time?"

I shook my head. "No. It was just really busy before the holidays."

"Well, you're here now and you can do nothing but rest and relax," she said brightly as she led me into the kitchen.

"Thank you again, Stephanie. Are you sure it's okay that I'm a couple days early?"

"Of course it is!" She took two mugs out of the cupboard and placed a tea bag in each before pouring water from the kettle into both mugs. "You know you're welcome to visit anytime you want. Besides, it's nice to have you here early. The rest of the family won't be arriving until Christmas Eve day so this will give you a couple of days to just take it easy and get caught up on your sleep. It'll be a nice vacation for you."

"I'm not going to sit on my ass doing nothing," I protested. "I can help you with baking or cleaning or whatever it is – "

"Nonsense!" She said briskly. "I don't need help with anything and don't take this the wrong way, honey, but you really do look like you're going to fall over. Here, drink your tea and then you can have a nice, long nap."

I smiled at her and sat down in the chair before taking a sip of the fragrant tea. I was suddenly very glad I had come to the cabin. Despite the fact that it was close to Aiden's cabin, despite the fact that Stephanie and Joe were Aiden's friends, I felt more calm sitting at the table with Stephanie then I had in weeks.

"Now," Stephanie took her own sip of tea, "tell me what's been happening with that fellow, Jamie, at work. Aiden was here last weekend and he told us that this new guy had a crush on you. He wasn't too happy about it either." She grinned.

I flushed and shook my head. "Nothing's going on. I mean, he's asked me out a couple of times, but I haven't said yes yet."

"Why not?"

"I'm not so sure it's a good idea to date someone I work with."

"I suppose not. Not to mention that Aiden clearly disapproves of it. He's such a stick in the mud." She laughed her tinkling little laugh. "Speaking of crushes – Aiden has a crush on you. You know that right?"

"He doesn't," I said immediately. "He absolutely does not."

She shrugged. "He talks about you all the time – it's why I thought you two were dating when I first met you. And he's never brought a woman up to his cabin before. In fact, the other day I was asking Joe if he could ever remember meeting one of Aiden's lady friends and he said no."

"He brought me to the cabin because my dog died and he was a total dick about it. He was trying to apologize for being an asshat."

Stephanie laughed again. "You know, I find it so hard to believe that Aiden is an asshat. He's always been so sweet to us."

"Count yourself lucky," I muttered. "I've had to distract multiple coworkers from trying to murder him in his office."

"Well then I guess he's lucky to have you, isn't he?" Stephanie grinned.

"Yeah, maybe mention that to him the next time you see him," I groused.

"I can do that, honey," she laughed. "So, are you not dating this Jamie because of the co-worker thing or because you've got a crush on Aiden?"

"I don't have a crush on Aiden," I protested.

"Please, honey. He doesn't have a crush on you, you don't have a crush on him...blah, blah, blah. You could hardly keep your eyes off of each other the entire time you were here. Plus did I mention that he talks about you all the time? Lina did this and Lina said that..."

She chuckled to herself. "Joe's been calling him a love-struck schoolboy."

"We just work together," I said loudly. I could feel my cheeks heating up and my heart was beating too heavily in my chest. "I keep telling you that there's nothing going on between us, Stephanie. Nothing!"

She gave me a startled look. "I'm sorry, honey. I didn't mean to upset you with my teasing. Sometimes I don't know when to stop."

I immediately felt ashamed of my reaction and I reached out and squeezed her hand. "No, I'm sorry. I'm just – it's been a long week and I'm just feeling the stress of the holidays."

She squeezed my hand back. "Well, these next few days will be the best medicine for you. Now, finish up your tea and then I'll tuck you into bed for a nap."

"Thank you, Stephanie." I was dangerously close to tears again and she patted my hand gently.

"You're welcome, honey."

* * *

"Steph? Where are you, sugar?" Joe's loud voice boomed through the cabin.

"In here, honey!" Stephanie sang out.

It was two days later. Despite Stephanie's protests, I was in the kitchen helping her with some last-minute baking. I had done nothing but sleep and sit curled up by the fire for the last two days and I felt much better. I hummed a Christmas carol under my breath as I rolled out the dough for the pie crust.

Joe stuck his head into the kitchen. "What smells so good?"

"That's the pumpkin pie." Stephanie winked at him as he patted her bottom.

There was a familiar bark and I whipped around, my stomach dropping to my knees when King came bounding into the kitchen. His tail wagging madly, he made a beeline straight for me and stood on his hind legs. He placed his front legs on my shoulders and licked my face enthusiastically.

I sputtered and pushed ineffectively at him. "King, down!"

He ignored me, his tail thumping against the cupboards as he licked my face repeatedly. A hand wrapped around his collar and Aiden pulled him away. He smacked him lightly on the rump and frowned at him. "King, down. Now."

King, panting happily, dropped to his belly and gazed adoringly at me as Aiden said apologetically, "I'm sorry, Lina."

I gave him a strained smile before turning away. Behind me, I could hear Stephanie giving Aiden a hug and kiss to the cheek before Joe clapped him on the back.

"Come out to the barn, Aiden. I want to show you the new horse Steph bought me for Christmas."

The two of them, followed by King, left the kitchen and I took a deep breath. My stomach was churning and I swallowed thickly as Stephanie, humming quietly, stirred the batter for the cookies.

"What is Aiden doing here, Stephanie?" I said abruptly.

"We invited him for Christmas. His parents went to Jamaica this year and I couldn't stand the thought of him spending Christmas alone."

She licked the batter from her fingers. "Did I forget to mention that to you?"

"Yes," I said.

She paused and gave me a thoughtful look. "What's wrong, honey?"

"Nothing." I continued to roll out the pastry and Stephanie touched my shoulder lightly.

"Are you sure? It looks like you're trying to roll the pastry right through the counter."

I stopped and took a deep breath. "No, I'm fine. Really."

"Are you sure? Because I – "

"Mom? We're here!"

The front door slammed and Stephanie gave me a delighted look. "The kids are here! Come on, Lina, I want you to meet everyone."

I followed Stephanie down the hallway and into the living room. A man, the spitting image of Joe, swept her into his embrace and hugged her tightly as a small blonde woman and two pre-teen boys watched.

"Hi, mom."

"Hello, honey." She kissed his cheek. "Lina, this is our oldest, Joe Junior, and his wife Ellie and their two boys Jonathan and Matthew."

"It's nice to meet you." I shook Joe's hand as Stephanie embraced Ellie and the boys.

"Where's your sister?" Stephanie asked.

"They were right behind us. I imagine they'll be here any – "

The door opened, there was the sound of children laughing, and a young boy and girl ran into the room.

"Grandma!" They launched themselves at Stephanie and she laughed and hugged them both.

"Look at you two! I swear you've grown a foot since I last saw you!"

"It's all the Christmas baking they've been eating." A short, balding man entered the room and smiled affectionately at the kids. "Maddie, Tyson, take your coats off and hang them in the closet, please."

They ran out of the room and the man smiled at Stephanie. "Hi, Stephanie."

"Hi, Steve. It's good to see you." She hugged him tightly as a woman, her hair dark like Joe's but her complexion pale like Stephanie's, entered the room.

"Beth!" Stephanie kissed her cheek. "Beth, Steve, this is our friend Lina. Lina, this is my oldest daughter Beth and her husband Steve, and these two little rugrats," she hugged the kids who had stampeded back into the room sans jackets, "are Madison and Tyson."

"Nice to meet you." I shook Steve's hand as Beth put her arm around Stephanie's shoulders.

"We have a surprise for you, mom."

"You do?" Stephanie grinned. "I love surprises."

"We know." Beth laughed before turning her mother toward the doorway. A young woman, her dark eyes sparkling, was standing there and Stephanie gasped loudly.

"Susan?"

"Hi, mom!"

Tears flowing down her cheeks, Stephanie pulled the woman into her embrace and smothered her face with kisses. "What are you doing here? I thought you were staying in London for the holidays."

Susan smiled and squeezed her hand. "I was but I decided last minute that I wanted to come home."

"I'm so glad you're here," Stephanie whispered. She hugged the young woman again before turning back to the others. "Who wants hot chocolate?"

* * *

"So, Lina, how do you know mom and dad?" Ellie smiled at me.

"We met her through Aiden," Stephanie replied. She was holding Madison on her lap and the little girl grinned up at her before taking another sip of hot chocolate.

"Are you dating Aiden?" Susan asked quickly.

"God, no," I replied. "I work for him, actually."

"What do you do at the firm?" Ellie asked curiously.

"I'm his assistant."

"Do you enjoy it?"

"It's a good job." I smiled at her.

"Aiden's always going on and on about how wonderful she is. Best assistant he's ever had, he said," Stephanie said. "Your father and I were so happy to finally meet her. She's delightful."

I flushed as Stephanie blew a kiss to me.

"Where is dad anyway?" Joe asked.

"Oh, he's out in the barn with Aiden. I imagine they'll be back any minute now."

"Aiden's here?" Susan sat up straight and smoothed down her hair.

"Yes." Stephanie gave her a loving look tinged with exasperation. "Behave yourself please, Susan."

"I always do, mom." She grinned at her before standing. "Excuse me, please."

She disappeared from the room as Beth rolled her eyes. "Poor Aiden. I bet if he knew Susan was going to be here, he wouldn't have come."

She glanced at me. "Susan's had a crush on Aiden for years."

"Who knows, maybe this year Susan will get her Christmas wish and find Aiden under the tree wearing nothing but a bow." Joe snickered as Ellie smacked him lightly on the arm.

"Joe, behave yourself!"

Joe grinned at her. "Listen, Aiden's only human and he hasn't had a girlfriend in years. Susan's like a bulldog, man. She's going to wear him down eventually."

He laughed loudly and I forced myself to smile as the rest of the room joined in. In truth, I was feeling sick to my stomach. I took a deep breath as the front door opened and a blast of cold air swept into the living room. I was sitting in the oversized armchair next to the fireplace with a blanket wrapped around my legs, and I cringed when King came bounding into the room. He was covered in snow and he shook his body, drool and snow splattering onto the floor as Madison and Tyson giggled and patted his broad body. He licked them once before spotting me. He woofed softly and I made a loud, distinctly unladylike grunt when he leaped onto my lap.

He licked my face and I pushed his head down. "King, enough."

He squished his butt down between the chair and my legs before resting his upper body across my lap. I pushed at his body but it was like trying to move a rock and I gave up with a soft sigh as Joe and Aiden walked into the living room.

"King, down." Aiden frowned.

King, panting happily, ignored him completely before licking the side of my head. I wiped the drool from my ear as Aiden frowned again.

"King, down. Right now."

"It's fine. I don't mind." I stroked King's head and the dog sighed deeply and rested his chin on my arm before closing his eyes.

Steve laughed. "He certainly seems to like you."

"Yeah." I made another soft grunt when Madison and Tyson climbed into the armchair and draped their small bodies across King's. They patted him and stroked his ears as his tail thumped happily against my leg. I tried to breathe shallowly and wondered if I would actually hear the sound of my ribs snapping under the kids' and King's combined weight.

Joe and Aiden were making the rounds, hugging and shaking hands with the others, and I smiled at Tyson as he leaned over the dog and stared at me.

"You're pretty," he announced.

I laughed. "Thanks. You're very handsome."

"I know. I'm only five and I already have a girlfriend."

"You do? What's her name?"

"Mindy. We're in kindergarten together."

"That's nice." I winced as King shifted and one of his nails dug into my thigh.

Aiden dropped into the armchair on the other side of the fireplace and frowned at me. "You're being crushed, Lina. King doesn't need to sit on your lap. He – "

"Hello, Aiden."

A look of apprehension crossed his face before he masked it with a polite smile. "Susan! I didn't know you were going to be here. I thought you were in London."

I watched as Susan nearly skipped across the room. She had changed into a tight low-cut shirt and jeans that I was pretty sure she had to oil herself up to get into. Her body was amazing, tight and firm, and absolutely nothing jiggled as she hurried toward Aiden. She had combed her hair and applied makeup and I realized with dismay that the girl was stunning.

Jealousy, strong and unpleasant, flowed through me when she plopped herself down on Aiden' lap and kissed him firmly on the mouth.

"Aren't you happy to see me?" She pouted prettily as Aiden gave her a strained smile.

"I am. How's London?"

"So great." She smoothed her hand down his chest. "I've been having a really great time."

"Good." He shifted uncomfortably under her and Stephanie cleared her throat.

"There's another chair right beside me, honey."

"I know," Susan said cheerfully. She continued to sit on Aiden's lap as he glanced quickly at me. I kept the polite, disinterested look on my face but inside I was nearly seething with jealousy. I wanted to stalk over there and yank Susan off of his lap by her long, soft hair. I took a deep breath and shook off the image of me punching Susan in the face. I outweighed her by at least a hundred pounds. How difficult would it be to pound her into oblivion for touching Aiden? Not that difficult, I decided.

Tyson had crawled over King and was leaning against my chest. He smiled up at me and patted my face before resting his head against my shoulder. I tried not to wince. I had a bruise from where Aiden bit me that night in his office, and I tried to subtly move so that Tyson's head wasn't resting directly against it.

He lifted his head and squinted at my neck before pushing the neckline of my t-shirt to the side. "What's that?"

He pointed to the bruise as Stephanie frowned.

"Oh honey, what happened?"

"Uh, I ran into the doorframe in the middle of the night," I lied quickly. "Serves me right for not turning on the light."

I pulled my t-shirt out of Tyson's hands and quickly covered the bruise before glancing at Aiden. He was staring at me with a sick look on his face and I gave him a curious look.

Susan cleared her throat loudly. "If I had known you were spending Christmas with us, Aiden, I would have brought the present I bought you in London."

"You didn't have to buy me anything," Aiden replied. He shifted again before asking politely, "How's the teaching job going?"

"Oh great, great!" Susan enthused. "I love my kids."

She turned and smiled at me. "I teach gymnastics. I used to be a professional gymnast. Almost made it to the Olympics a few years ago."

Shit. A gymnast.

I didn't have a chance of winning a catfight with her, she'd be solid muscle and bendy as hell. Besides, it didn't matter. Given a choice between a gymnast and my fat ass, what man wouldn't want to bang the goddamn gymnast? I plucked self-consciously at my t-shirt that was clinging to my round belly and gave her a faint smile.

"Wow! Congratulations."

"Thanks!" She started to settle more firmly on to Aiden's lap and squeaked in surprise when he twisted out from beneath her and stood.

"Sorry." He gave her an apologetic smile. "But I've really got to rescue Lina from King. He's going to crush her ribcage."

He moved toward me and lifted first Madison and then Tyson off of King's broad back before taking King's collar. He pulled firmly. "King, down."

The dog made a snort of displeasure but jumped down obediently before lying in front of the fire.

I took a deep breath and unfolded my legs from the chair. "Thanks."

I winced as I rubbed at my ribcage and then blinked in shock when Aiden dropped into the chair beside me. The armchair was large but he was a big man and I was no delicate flower. I twitched when he slid his hands under my ass and shifted me until I was half sitting on the chair and half-sitting on his lap.

"Comfortable?" He gave me a smile tinged with desperation and I hesitated before nodding and relaxing against him.

"Sure am."

"There's another chair by mom," Susan said sweetly. "I'm sure that would be more comfortable for you, Lina. We wouldn't want Aiden to be the one with the crushed ribcage, now would we?"

That's it. I don't care if she's a gymnast – I'm kicking her tight little ass.

As if sensing my thoughts, Aiden slid his hand under my hair and gripped the back of my neck, holding me firmly in place as Stephanie said sharply, "Susan!"

Susan glanced at her mother. "What?"

Stephanie gave her a pointed look, her pale face was flushed with anger, and Susan sighed before looking back at us. A small frown line appeared between her eyes. Aiden was kneading and rubbing the back of my neck, and she smiled stiffly at us as Stephanie clapped her hands briskly.

"Who wants more hot chocolate?"

Chapter 9

"Lina, c'mere for a minute." Tyson tugged on my pants and I dried my hands before following him to the doorway of the kitchen.

"What's up, little man?"

"Just um, stand here." He positioned me in the doorway as Beth laughed quietly.

He gave me a nervous look and I ruffled his hair. "What can I do for you, buddy?"

"Look up," he said shyly.

I glanced above me, a smile breaking out on my face, at the plant hanging from the doorway.

"Do you know what that is?" Tyson asked eagerly. He held my hand in a sweaty little grip and I winked at him.

"Why don't you tell me what it is?"

"It's mistletoe!" He crowed. "You have to kiss me now – it's tradition!"

"So it is." I bent down and winked again at him. "Pucker up, little man."

He pursed his lips and I kissed him quickly on the mouth before straightening. He giggled and hugged me around the waist. "I like you, Lina."

"I like you too, Tyson."

Beth picked up a tray of veggies in one hand and held out her other to Tyson. "Okay, Romeo, come back to the living room with me."

He took her hand and stared eagerly at me. "Are you coming, Lina?"

"I sure am. Just give me a couple of minutes," I replied.

"Okay." He followed Beth down the hallway and I sighed and leaned against the doorframe before closing my eyes. I rubbed my forehead wearily. I had the beginning of a tension headache and I wondered if there was any way in hell I could fake some kind of emergency and get my ass out of here. I wanted to go home, crawl into my bed, and forget all about Christmas and Aiden and –

"Lina?"

I jerked and opened my eyes. Aiden was standing in the doorway staring at me in concern. "Are you okay?"

"Fine," I replied shortly. "Did you know they invited me for Christmas?"

He hesitated and then nodded. "Yeah, they mentioned it to me."

"Why didn't you tell me they invited you as well?" I scowled at him.

"Because I knew you wouldn't come and I wanted to see you," he said simply.

I sighed and rubbed at my forehead again. "What the hell for?"

"I owe you an apology. Actually," his brow darkened, "I owe you three apologies."

"Oh yeah?"

He nodded. "I'm sorry for what I said to you in the office. You don't belong to me, and I had no right to question you about your relationship with Parker."

I didn't reply and he cleared his throat. "I also wanted to apologize for earlier. I said I wouldn't touch you again and then I did. I, uh, was a bit desperate to get away from Susan."

I snorted. "Yes, because it sucks so much to have a hot, beautiful gymnast practically begging you to fuck her. Poor Aiden. It must be so taxing to have gorgeous women throwing themselves at you all the time."

He blushed. "Putting aside the fact that she's my best friend's daughter, she's not my type."

"Of course she isn't. No man wants a chick who can bounce a quarter off her ass and put her legs behind her head. That's just ridiculous," I scoffed.

"I don't want her," he insisted before repeating himself, "She's not my type."

"What is your type? Hmm?" I scowled at him.

"You."

I swallowed looked away from his dark eyes. "Sorry, I don't do the 'wham, bam, thank you, ma'am' thing."

"I know," he sighed.

There was a moment of silence between us before I glanced up at him again. "What's the third apology?"

He reached out and pulled gently on the top of my t-shirt. The sick look returned to his face as he studied the bruise.

"This," he said hoarsely. "I'm so sorry, princess. I didn't realize I had bitten you so hard. I was feeling a little crazy that night and I took it too far."

I studied him carefully. His face was ashen and he couldn't stop staring at the bruise on my soft flesh.

"Aiden? Hey, Aiden?" I touched his face gently and he shuddered all over before raising his gaze to mine.

"It's not that big of a deal. Really."

"You're bruised," he whispered.

"I bruise easily," I replied. "Always have. You should see the ones on my ass." I tried to joke with him and groaned inwardly when his eyes widened.

"Fuck! I'm a goddamn idiot. I should have discussed with you a safe word or something."

"Even if we had discussed a safe word beforehand, I wouldn't have used it," I said earnestly. "It didn't hurt at the time and I – I liked it."

Desire flared in his eyes and my body responded immediately. I could feel my nipples hardening and I rubbed my thighs together in an effort to ease the sudden ache between them. I stared into his eyes before licking my lips, and he groaned and looked away.

"Don't look at me that way, princess," he warned hoarsely. His hands were closed into tight fists and he took a step back.

"What way?" I whispered.

"Like you want me to fuck you," he muttered.

My entire body was throbbing now. The noise of the others in the living room had faded away completely and I studied Aiden's mouth, remembering how firm his lips were, how warm his mouth was against mine. With madness singing her sweet song in my ear, I stepped closer until my breasts brushed against his chest.

He groaned loudly and reached to cup them before dropping his hands back to his side. I pressed my belly against his erection and smiled up at him.

"Look up, Aiden."

He looked up obediently and I traced my hand over his broad chest.

"It's mistletoe."

"Yeah," he replied in a low throaty groan.

"You have to kiss me. It's tradition," I whispered.

He stared down at me, his gaze nearly setting me on fire with lust. "Lina – "

"Kiss me, Aiden."

With another low groan, he bent his head and touched his mouth to mine. I parted my lips immediately, wrapping my arms around his neck as he moved his hands around my waist and drew me up against his hard body. I stood on my tip toes and pressed my breasts into his hard chest.

He kissed me softly, his lips coaxing and his tongue gentle as he drew my tongue into his mouth. He sucked lightly on it before tracing my lips with the tip of his tongue. I moaned into his mouth. Aiden had never kissed me like this before. He was treating me like I was a fragile flower and although there was a part of me that enjoyed his gentleness, I missed my demanding and rough Aiden.

"Harder," I muttered against his lips. "Kiss me harder, Aiden."

"Lina, I don't want to – "

I cut off his comment by thrusting my tongue into his mouth. I kissed him hard, trying to force him to kiss me back in the way that I wanted and, after a moment, he was taking my mouth in hard, biting nips and licks.

I sighed happily as he ravaged my mouth. This was the Aiden I wanted, the Aiden I needed. I wanted him to be demanding, to push me to my limits and to take what belonged to him. I could try and deny it all I wanted but he was right. I was his.

We sprang apart guiltily when Stephanie cleared her throat. Gasping, my face bright red and my knees shaking, I stared wild-eyed at her.

"Sorry to interrupt," she said cheekily, "but I need to get dinner started."

"Of course," I said. "Excuse me, I just uh, need to freshen up and then I'll help you."

"Take your time, honey." She winked at me before squeezing Aiden's arm playfully.

Blushing furiously, I escaped down the hallway.

* * *

"That, sugar, was a delicious meal." Joe rubbed his belly and smiled at Stephanie.

She laughed. "Wait until tomorrow's dinner. It's even better."

I jumped up from the table and began to clear the dishes. Ellie and Beth soon joined in but Susan remained at the table. She had managed to snag a seat next to Aiden and she was nearly sitting on his lap. I picked up the bowl of carrots and ignored the jealousy I felt when Susan's hand slipped under the table. Aiden's eyes widened briefly and I knew without a doubt that she was grabbing his junk.

He moved his own hands under the table and a moment later Susan's were folded neatly on her own lap. She gave him a seductive pout and he frowned lightly at her before shifting his chair away from hers.

I sighed inwardly as I scraped the left-over carrots into a plastic container. Susan wasn't his type, Aiden had said so himself, so why was I so worried and disgruntled over her obvious flirting. If he hadn't slept with her yet, why did I think he would now?

"So, we need to discuss sleeping arrangements," Stephanie said suddenly. "Now that Susan is here, we're short a bed."

"I can sleep on the couch in the living room," I volunteered immediately.

Stephanie shook her head. "It's much too short, honey. You won't be comfortable at all."

"I don't mind, really," I replied.

"Aiden, you have the pull-out couch at your place, right?" Stephanie said innocently.

He nodded. "I do. Someone's more than welcome to use it."

"I'll sleep over at Aiden's place. It's my fault we don't have enough beds," Susan piped up before stroking Aiden's arm. "Thanks, Aiden. I really appreciate your hospitality."

Aiden gave Stephanie a decidedly panicked look and she shook her head.

"Honey, your father and I haven't seen you in months. We want you to stay here with us at the house. I'm sure Lina won't mind bunking at Aiden's place. Will you, honey?"

Aiden's gaze swung to mine and I almost giggled at the silent pleading in his eyes.

"Of course not." I smiled cheerfully at Stephanie. "If Aiden's okay with it. He sees me every day at work. He might want a break from my face."

"Nope. I'm happy to help out," Aiden said quickly. "But I was going to head back now and get the fire built up. It's supposed to be freezing tonight."

I swallowed heavily, remembering the last freezing night I had spent in Aiden's cabin, and snapped the lid on to the plastic container as Susan sighed loudly.

"Mom, I'll see you and dad plenty during the day. I don't see why I – "

"Susan, be a dear and help Ellie and Beth clean up so that Lina can gather her stuff to take to Aiden's, would you?"

"Sure," Susan muttered. She stood and I smiled briefly at her, ignoring my childish feeling of triumph, and hurried from the kitchen.

* * *

"You okay?" Aiden asked.

"Yeah," I puffed. The snow was deep and, busy staring at Aiden's ass, I had tripped and fallen flat on my face. I picked myself up and brushed the snow off my jacket before straightening my toque. "Just clumsy."

"Here, take my hand." He held his hand out and I took it gingerly as he shifted my suitcase in his other hand.

"I can take that." I reached for my suitcase and he shook his head.

"I've got it."

King barked loudly before bounding ahead of us. He plowed through the soft snow with his face and I laughed as we followed the path he made in the snow.

"Rex used to love the snow." I smiled at Aiden. "He would run like crazy through it at the dog park and roll around. I called it his 'Rex Angels'."

Aiden squeezed my hand. "Are you going to get another dog, Lina?"

"Yes. I wasn't sure at first but I miss having a dog. I'll go to the animal shelter after Christmas and find one that needs a home."

"You're a good person," Aiden said suddenly.

I laughed. "Adopting a dog from the shelter doesn't make me a good person, Aiden."

"It does," he replied.

We walked silently for a few minutes. Thanks to the moonlight and snow, it was easy to see the cabin looming ahead of us.

"Thanks for your help back there," Aiden said gratefully.

"What do you mean?"

"I mean for agreeing to stay at my place instead of Susan. I know you wanted to use the holidays to get away from me for a while." His face was carefully neutral.

I sighed. "Aiden, it's not that I don't want to be around you. I just – I don't think it's a good idea for us to socialize outside of work. You don't want a relationship and I'm not looking for a fling with my boss. Besides, I'm not that great in the sack and I'd like to leave our sexual adventures on a high note." I winked at him, trying to get him to laugh.

He glared at me at his hand tightened on mine. "You're not terrible in bed, Lina. I hate it when you say that. Your ex-boyfriend is a dick for saying you were."

I returned his scowl. "Fucking me twice doesn't qualify you to make that statement."

"But your ex can say whatever he wants," he said.

I shrugged. "Kent was with me for four years, Aiden. He knows exactly what – "

"Yeah, I know," he interrupted. "Stop talking about it, would you? You have no idea how angry it makes me to think about that asshole touching you."

He snorted with disgust. "Kent. What kind of fucking name is Kent? I guarantee you that someone named Kent doesn't have a clue what he's doing in bed."

I giggled despite myself and the corners of Aiden's mouth turned up. "Did he know you faked your orgasms?"

I blushed and looked away. "No."

"See," he said smugly, "I told you Kent doesn't have a fucking clue. Did you ever have a real orgasm with him?"

"Aiden, this isn't an appropriate conversation for an employee to have with her boss."

"I've been inside you, Ms. Jones," he said dryly. "I think we're past the usual employee/employer chit-chat, don't you?"

I sighed loudly and he squeezed my hand again. "Did you?"

"In the beginning of the relationship, yeah," I replied. "But after about a year, it started to bother Kent that I had to be touching myself or that he had to touch me while we were having sex, and he didn't understand why I couldn't come from just having sex. I was tired of hearing about women who could orgasm from sex alone so I started faking them. It was easier that way."

"So you faked your orgasms for nearly four years?" He shook his head. "Jesus, that sucks."

I laughed again. "It wasn't that bad, Aiden. My best friend, Tracy, bought me a vibrator when I confessed to her that I was faking them. After that, whenever Kent was working late, I had some, um, playtime with myself."

I was blushing and I couldn't believe what I was saying to Aiden but I couldn't seem to stop the words from spilling out of my mouth.

"Actually," I continued, "I think good old Phil was the final straw that broke the proverbial camel's back."

"Phil?" Aiden laughed. "You named your vibrator Phil?"

"Well, Phillip actually, but I usually just call him Phil."

Aiden laughed again and my heart warmed at the sound.

"What happened?" He prompted.

"Kent was working late so I headed to bed with Phil. Only Kent didn't have to work nearly as late as he usually did, and he came home to find me naked in the bed with Phil working his magic while I thought about – "

I clamped my mouth shut in horror. I had been about two seconds away from telling Aiden that I had been thinking about him while I masturbated with my damn vibrator.

"Thought about what?" He asked curiously.

"Oh, you know, the usual celebrities – Chris Hemsworth, Ryan Reynolds," I lied cheerfully.

"Of course." He rolled his eyes. "What happened when Kent found you with Phil?"

I snickered. I should have been mortified that my boss was talking about my vibrator but it was actually pretty damn funny when you thought about it.

"He was not pleased, as you can imagine. I had to listen to a two-hour lecture about how I had humiliated and emasculated him. About a week later, he packed his stuff, told me he was leaving until I lost some weight and figured out what the hell I was doing in bed, and I haven't heard from him since."

We were just outside the front door of Aiden's cabin now, and when Aiden stood there silently I reached for the door handle. He dropped my suitcase in the snow and pushed me up against the door, pressing his body against mine.

I stared up at him, my throat going dry at the look in his eyes, as he leaned down. "Do you know what I would have done if I had come home to find you naked with a vibrator, Ms. Jones?"

"No," I squeaked out. There was no way I should have been able to feel his erection through our layers of clothing but there it was. Hot and heavy and pushing against my stomach.

He leaned closer still, until his mouth was at my ear and his hot breath was sending shivers down my spine. "I would have made you fuck yourself with the vibrator while I put you on your hands and knees and fucked that gorgeous, tight ass."

I moaned loudly, my knees weakening at the image that shot through my head, and Aiden gave me a hard grin. "Did that idiot of a boyfriend ever fuck you in the ass, Ms. Jones?"

"No." My voice was hoarse and I cleared my throat nervously. "No, I – he wanted to but I wouldn't let him."

"Why not?"

"I don't know."

"Were you afraid it would hurt?"

"No. Kent wasn't very uh – big." I licked my lips. "You're much bigger than him."

He grinned down at me. "You are seriously good for my ego, Ms. Jones."

"You're welcome."

His grin widened for a moment before he gave me a thoughtful look. "If I wanted to fuck you in the ass, would you let me?"

"We're – we're not together," I replied breathlessly. The thought of Kent invading my ass had made my insides roll with nausea but thinking about Aiden taking me there, imagining how it would feel to be on my hands and knees and helpless to stop him as he slid his cock into my ass, was making me embarrassingly wet.

"Yes, I know," he said with a touch of irritation as his hand moved to the back of my neck and gripped it firmly. "But if we were - if you were mine and in my bed every night - would you let me fuck your ass?"

I swallowed loudly. "Yes."

His nostrils flared and his hand tightened on my neck. "You're making it very difficult to resist you, Ms. Jones."

His gaze dropped to my mouth and it was all I could do not to kiss him. Feeling like I was making the wrong decision, I pushed lightly on his chest.

"We shouldn't do this, Aiden. It will end badly. We both know that."

"Yeah," he said.

It was only slightly warmer in the cabin and I kept my jacket and mittens on as Aiden built up the fire. He carried my suitcase into the bedroom and I gave him an alarmed look when he returned dragging the top mattress from the bed.

"I'll sleep on the couch," he said gruffly. "It's too cold for either of us to sleep in the bedroom alone."

"I'll sleep on the couch," I said firmly. "You'll be too uncomfortable."

"It's fine. I don't – "

"No," I interrupted. "There isn't enough room with the mattress to pull out the couch and I'm shorter than you. I'll take the couch."

He scowled but didn't argue as he dropped the mattress in front of the fire. King, his tongue lolling from his mouth, squeezed into the small space between the fireplace and the mattress and rested his head on his paws with a soft sigh.

"So, what did you want to do now?" Aiden asked.

I licked my lips again. What I wanted to do was strip naked, lie down on the mattress and invite Aiden to do all sorts of deliciously naughty things to me. Instead, I gave him a nervous smile. "I'm pretty tired. I think I'll just change and go to bed. If that's okay with you?"

He nodded and studied a spot on the wall behind me. "That's fine."

I left the living room and stood in the cold bedroom, my limbs shaking and my hands turning numb as I contemplated whether or not to take off my bra.

For Pete's sake, you ninny! He's seen you braless before. Just change and get back out there before you freeze to death.

Moving quickly, I stripped out of my clothes and changed into my flannel pajamas. My feet were freezing and I kept my thick socks on before throwing my hoodie on and heading back to the living room.

Aiden was already lying on the mattress. The covers were pooled around his waist and I looked away quickly from his broad, naked chest wondering if the rest of him was just as naked.

Climb under the covers and find out, girl. You want him and he wants you. Denying yourself what you want is ridiculous.

I shrugged out of my hoodie, ignoring the way Aiden's eyes dropped to my chest under my loose flannel top, and climbed under the blankets on the couch. I rested my head on the pillow and stared blankly at the ceiling.

Aiden thinks I'm good in bed. If I keep sleeping with him, he'll realize the truth sooner or later and if you think it was humiliating that Kent believed you sucked in bed, how do you think it will feel when Aiden believes that?

Aiden could teach you to be better. He's obviously more experienced then Kent. Maybe all you need is the right person to show you what to do. Plus, you've been doing yoga. You're way bendier now.

Not bendy enough for what he'll undoubtedly want.

Arguing with myself was beginning to feel like something a crazy person would do and I cut off the voice in my head with an abruptness that surprised me. It was pointless to keep sleeping with him. Even if I managed to keep his interest between the sheets, where exactly would this lead? Nowhere, that's where. Aiden wasn't interested in a relationship and he especially wasn't interested in having one with an employee.

Are you sure? He certainly can't seem to keep his hands off of you.

That was true but lust had a way of making people do crazy things.

So be crazy for once. Do something that doesn't make sense, that you know is wrong. Stop being a scared little mouse and just let yourself have some fun. Sleep with Aiden. You're alone in a cabin with your super-hot, super-sexy boss and he's most likely naked under those sheets. Do you really want to waste that opportunity? Put on your big girl panties and let yourself have a casual, no-commitment-required fling for the first time in your life. You deserve it. It's Christmas for God's sake!

I sat up straight and stared at the flames. "You're right," I announced. "Merry fucking Christmas to me."

Aiden twisted his head to stare at me curiously. "Lina, are you okay?"

"It's Christmas," I replied.

"Uh, yes. I know." He gave me an odd look as I snickered loudly.

"What's wrong? Are you too cold?" He asked.

I nodded. "Definitely too cold." I threw back the blankets, slid off the couch and tried, unsuccessfully, to crawl sexily onto the mattress.

"What are you doing, Lina?" Aiden asked carefully.

"I'm cold, Aiden. I want you to warm me up." I wiggled under the blankets as he sat up and inched away.

"This isn't a good idea, remember? You said it yourself – it will only end badly."

I shrugged as I eased my hand under the covers. I was itching to find out if he was naked.

"Only if we allow it to. I want you, you want me – we're all alone in the cabin. Why shouldn't we take advantage of that?"

"Lina – "

"Be quiet, Aiden," I interrupted. "I don't want anything from you after this. Okay? I know exactly what you want from me and for tonight, hell for the rest of the holidays, that's what I want too."

"And after?" He asked quietly.

I shrugged. "After, we go back to the way it was."

"This is a very bad idea," he muttered as my hand bridged the gap between us and rested on his fabric-covered cock.

"Why aren't you naked?" I pouted.

"Why aren't you?" He countered. His breath hissed out between his teeth when I stroked him firmly.

"Good point." It was time to ditch the seriously unsexy flannel look I was sporting.

I reached for the buttons on my shirt and Aiden covered my hand with his.

"Are you sure, Lina? Absolutely sure that this is what you want?" He gave me a searching look.

"Yes," I said firmly. "Make your decision, Aiden. I'm not going to beg."

He gave me a dark look of desire. "Oh you'll beg, princess. I guarantee it."

I shuddered with need as he unbuttoned my shirt. "Someone's awfully full of himself."

He grinned and tugged off my shirt before tossing it on the floor. "You like my confidence."

"It's mildly attractive," I admitted begrudgingly.

He was staring at the bruise on my shoulder and I touched his face lightly. "Hey? I bruise easily, remember? It's no big deal."

He leaned forward and pressed a soft kiss against my bruised flesh. I moaned lightly, my hands tightening on his biceps as he licked it with his warm tongue.

"I hate that I hurt you," he whispered.

"You're not a very good Dom, Aiden. One little bruise and you're flipping out," I teased lightly.

He shook his head. "One – a good Dom would never lose control and bruise their sub like this and two – I'm not a Dom."

"Of course you're not." I rolled my eyes.

"I'm not," he insisted.

"So you're telling me you'd let me tie you to the bedposts and ride you like a pony if I wanted?"

"Yes."

I blinked in surprise. "Put a collar and cuffs on you? Poor hot wax on your chest? Spank you?"

I had run out of things that, admittedly, my limited knowledge of BDSM could come up with and I raised my eyebrows expectantly at him.

"Yes, no, and yes."

"No hot wax, huh? Chicken," I scoffed.

He laughed and placed another gentle kiss on my shoulder. "I don't like to hurt and I don't like to be hurt."

"Spanking hurts."

"In a good way."

"Have you been spanked before?"

"No. I'm usually the spanker."

"Surprise, surprise," I replied. "Why did you say yes to it then?"

"Because all that's important to me is making you feel good, Lina. If tying me up or spanking me turns you on, I'll do it."

I stared silently at him. Truthfully, I had no idea what to say to that. The idea that a man would be willing to do whatever in bed just to make me happy had never occurred to me. It had always been about what Kent wanted and I didn't know what to do with this new information.

He kissed me softly on the mouth. "I'll do all of those things, Lina, but I have a feeling that what you really want is for me to do all of those things to you."

A sweet pang of lust swept through my body. Aiden was right, I did want those things, and I gave him a weak smile. "It's kind of difficult to do all of that in just a few days."

He nodded. "Yes, I suppose you're right. We do have a limited window, so why exactly are we still talking and not fucking?"

"You tell me," I whispered before kissing him.

He groaned and returned my kiss before kneading lightly at my breast. His fingers pulled firmly at my nipple and I arched my back and put my arms around his broad shoulders, tugging him closer.

"Lie back, Lina," he whispered.

I relaxed on the mattress as he grasped the waistband of my flannel pajama bottoms. "Hips up."

I lifted and he tugged the bottoms and my panties down my legs and off my feet. He touched the thick socks I wore and smiled at me. "Feet still cold?"

I nodded and then moaned loudly when he lifted my leg and traced the back of my calf with his warm tongue. He kissed my shin and my knee before pressing another one against the top of my thigh. He tried to push my legs apart, frowning when I resisted.

"Open your legs, princess."

"Aiden, I'm not really comfortable with what you're about to do."

"What am I about to do?"

I flushed and waved my hand vaguely in the direction of my crotch. "You know."

"Say it," he said.

My flush deepened and I looked away from his steady gaze. "Um, taste me?"

"Such a polite little princess," he said in amusement. "I really need to change that."

He pressed his large body between my lower legs and I clenched my knees together. "Aiden, I haven't showered since this morning."

"So?" He traced circles around my tightly closed knees before licking the top of my thigh again.

I stared at him in frustration. Why was he being deliberately obtuse? "So, I need to um, freshen up, first."

"Why?" He tasted the freckle he found on the outside of my knee.

"Just let me have a quick shower," I begged. "Five minutes, that's all I need."

"I don't want to taste soap, Lina. I want to taste you," he replied.

I stared uncertainly at him. Kent hadn't gone down on me very often but each time he had insisted I shower first. Even then, there was always a mild look of distaste on his face both before and after. After a while, the five minutes he would spend down there hadn't seemed worth the worry and embarrassment that I smelled or tasted strange and I had stopped requesting it.

"Aiden, I – "

"I can smell you," he said suddenly. "Even with your legs so tightly closed, I can smell your sweet pussy and it," he dipped his head and inhaled deeply, "smells delicious."

"Oh my God," I groaned. My embarrassment had skyrocketed as soon as he said he could smell me and I tried to wiggle free of Aiden's tight grip.

"Please," I begged again. "Let me shower first. Please, Aiden."

He refused to release me and stared thoughtfully at me. "Did your ex-boyfriend," he paused before continuing dryly, "taste you, Lina?"

"Of course," I said nervously. No way, no how, was I telling Aiden I practically had to beg Kent for it. "Of course he did."

"How often?"

"I – what?" I stalled for time.

"How often did he *taste* you?" Aiden asked.

"Oh, uh, all the time," I lied.

"Kitten," he said warningly, "you know I'll spank you for lying to me."

A little tremor of lust went through me and my goddamn knees actually loosened a little at the thought. It didn't go unnoticed by Aiden and he grinned and slipped his fingers between my knees. I immediately clamped them shut again, trapping his hand, and he pressed his other arm across my tummy, preventing me from sitting up.

"How often," he asked again.

I sighed and stared at the ceiling. "Not that often."

"Once or twice a week?" He asked.

I didn't reply and he pulled his hand free from between my knees and traced his fingers up and down my outer thigh. "Once or twice a month?"

When I remained silent, he squeezed my hip warningly. "Answer me, Lina."

"Once every few months," I snapped. I was suddenly angry with Aiden for forcing me to reveal something so personal, so damn shameful, and I glared at him. "And even then, I had to beg him to do it. And he absolutely refused unless I showered first because I guess I smell or — or taste bad. There, are you happy, Aiden? Did you get the information you wanted?"

I was completely unprepared for the look of pity that crossed Aiden's face. No, I decided, not pity but sadness, maybe, with just a trace of anger?

"What — what's wrong?" I reached down and touched his dark hair. "Aiden, why are you looking at me like that?"

"Because I hate what that asshole has done to you," he said simply.

"He hasn't done anything to me," I said.

"He has," he sighed and that strange look of fleeting sadness crossed his face again. "Lina, listen very carefully to me, okay?"

I nodded and he smiled warmly at me. "I'm going to eat your pussy. In fact, I'm going to eat your pussy a tremendous amount of times over the next few days and if you insist on showering each time beforehand, you'll be in the shower all the damn time. Do you understand?"

"Aiden," I whispered, "I don't – "

"Do you understand?" He repeated.

I nodded and he smiled again before stroking my bare thighs soothingly. "I know you're feeling shy and uncomfortable and if you want to shower this time, I'll allow it. But," he pressed a warm kiss against my thigh, "what I really want is for you to trust me. To trust that nothing would please me more than tasting the sweetness of your pussy exactly as it is. Can you do that, Lina? Can you trust me?"

I stared at him for a long moment before relaxing my thighs. He smiled at me and I tingled all over when he kissed the inside of my thigh. "That's my good girl."

I stared at the ceiling and tried to relax as Aiden stretched out on his stomach between my thighs. I was incredibly nervous and tense and all of my previous desire had disappeared completely. When Aiden kissed the top of my pussy, nuzzling the dark curls, I jumped and made a short, anxious cry.

"Shh, kitten," he said. "It's going to feel so good, I promise."

I smiled weakly and returned my gaze to the ceiling as his thumbs massaged the crease between my thighs and my pussy.

Just relax, Lina. Just relax. Just let him kiss you for a few minutes, then you can fake your orgasm and he'll be satisfied.

He'll know if you fake your orgasm.

Shut up! He won't.

He will. You know he will. Then you'll get a spanking and – oh, hey, you know what? Go right ahead and fake that orgasm. Let's find out if he really can –

"Lina?"

I stopped the mental argument and glanced at Aiden. "What's wrong?"

"You're tensing up, princess."

I realized he was right. My thighs were pressing against Aiden's broad shoulders and my hands were tight fists in the sheets. I was nearly panting with anxiety and I took a few deep breaths as Aiden watched me silently. I was being ridiculous. It wasn't like I had never had a tongue in my pussy before.

No, but what if do you smell strange or taste bad? It's one thing for Kent to know that, quite another for Aiden. You really should shower.

"Aiden," my voice was quivering, "I think maybe I should – "

My voice cut out when Aiden bent his dark head and licked the swollen, wet lips of my pussy. It wasn't the hurried, tentative swipe I was used to. It was a slow, flat caress of his hot tongue that sent fire rocketing through my veins and a sudden and desperate need for more.

"OH!" I gasped loudly, my hips arching involuntarily into his mouth, and he rewarded me with another long, seductive lick.

"Oh, oh my gosh," I whispered.

"Lina?"

"Y-yeah," I stuttered as I stared wide-eyed at the ceiling. My entire body was vibrating and I desperately wanted him to lick me again.

"Look at me."

I forced my gaze to his. He was staring gravely at me and my pelvis jerked when he said, "Your pussy tastes so sweet – sweeter than the sweetest berry, Lina."

I stared wide-eyed at him as he pressed his big hands on the insides of my thighs. "Spread your legs nice and wide for me, kitten."

I let my legs fall open, his smile of approval sending shivers of delight up and down my spine, and closed my eyes as his dark head bent again. He licked my swollen lips before nibbling lightly on them and I moaned my approval. I was wide open to him, I could feel the cool air brushing over my clit, but he continued to tease and lick only the lips. His tongue felt incredible, hot and wet and delightfully soft, and I couldn't stop my pelvis from rising to meet each long caress.

It had already been well over five minutes and I realized with dismay that I needed to try and fake my orgasm. Aiden would be growing tired of tasting me and as good as his tongue felt, I was still too tense to let myself go completely. I took a deep breath and was about to let loose with a loud, hopefully convincing, moan when Aiden's wandering tongue brushed over my clit.

"Fuck!" I shouted and my hips bucked compulsively.

Aiden laughed, a low sound that vibrated against my pussy, and I blushed furiously when his gaze met mine. It wasn't that Kent hadn't licked my clit, he had, but this was somehow different. I couldn't even begin to explain it – all I knew was that I wanted him to do it again.

"Aiden," I whispered when he didn't move. "Please."

"Please what, kitten?"

"Please do that again."

He bent his head and licked my clit again. I cried out, my hands threading through his hair and clutching tightly, as he brushed my clit with delicate swipes of his tongue.

"Oh, oh my fucking God," I moaned. The most delicious and maddening tension was building in my stomach and I pulled compulsively at Aiden's hair when he sucked on my clit. I screamed loudly and ground my pussy against Aiden's hot mouth and tongue. One thick finger slid into my opening, its thrusting and pushing only inflaming me more, and I made an incoherent begging noise as Aiden sucked noisily at my swollen, hard clit.

When he stopped I made a harsh cry of need and tried to push his face back into my pussy. Jesus, his tongue and his mouth were amazing and I couldn't stop my needy cry when he lifted his head and grinned at me.

"Oh, Aiden, oh please, oh please," I begged shamelessly.

"Tell me what you want, princess."

"I – I want you to taste me again," I moaned.

He made a soft noise of disapproval. "Try again."

I bit my bottom lip and stared pleadingly at him. "Please?"

He pushed his finger deeper into my hot core and I thrust myself desperately against him.

"Tell me what I want to hear, kitten."

I couldn't say it. I couldn't but I had to. My decision to fake my orgasm had flown out the window and I was so close to the relief I craved. I wanted, *needed*, the real thing with a desperation I had never felt before.

"Please eat my pussy, Aiden," I said in a low voice.

"Louder, Lina."

"Please eat my pussy, Aiden!" I shouted it, not ashamed in the least of my begging, and Aiden rewarded me again by pushing my pussy lips apart with his thumbs and attacking my clit with his mouth and tongue.

I screamed hoarsely, my lower half arching off the mattress as I came explosively against Aiden's face. I writhed and moaned and shuddered as waves of pleasure washed over me until I collapsed against the mattress in a boneless little heap.

I was panting loudly, the blood roaring through my ears and my legs shuddering from the aftermath of my orgasm, and I forced my eyes open when I felt Aiden's hard body press against mine.

"Taste your sweetness, Lina," he murmured before kissing me deeply. I licked my taste from his tongue, my hands clutching at his broad back, as he kissed me for long moments. When he finally released my mouth, my lips were red and swollen and I was feeling dizzy from lack of oxygen.

"Aiden," I whispered, "oh my god, Aiden."

He grinned smugly at me before kissing the bruise on my shoulder. He licked my neck and nuzzled my ear before whispering, "You smell and taste delicious, Lina. I can't wait to eat your pussy every day."

I moaned as he settled himself in the cradle of my hips and his cock probed at my opening. He grasped one thigh and pulled my legs wider before pushing the head of his cock into my warmth.

"Ohhh," I sighed and dug my nails into his back as he pushed in further. When he was sheathed completely, he cupped my face and brushed his lips against my mouth.

"Look at me, Lina."

My eyelids fluttered open and I returned his smile. My entire body was still weak and tingling and I traced my hands along the hard muscles of his back.

"Did you like having your pussy eaten, princess?"

I blushed and nodded as he gave a little thrust with his hips.

"Say it."

"I – I liked having my pussy eaten," I whispered.

"I liked eating your pussy," he breathed into my ear as he began an easy slide and retreat motion. "You tasted so good, Lina. I've never tasted anyone as sweet as you."

I moaned quietly and he licked my bottom lip before whispering, "Tell me your pussy belongs to me."

I blinked at him and he made two hard thrusts that curled my toes into the mattress.

"Aiden – "

"Tell me, Lina," he said fiercely.

"My pussy belongs to you."

A hard grin of satisfaction crossed his face and I cried out when he propped himself above me and thrust roughly in and out. I braced my feet on the mattress and met each of his thrusts. Our hips slapped together in a rough rhythm as my pussy clung wetly to his thick cock.

He was starting to moan softly, his head twisting and his mouth dropping open as he drew closer to his climax. I watched in utter fascination as his head fell back and, with a harsh shout, he thrust a final time and his body arched against mine.

I rubbed his back and squeezed my inner muscles around him. He jerked and groaned loudly before collapsing against me. His breath stirred my hair and I closed my eyes and smiled happily. Aiden was heavy but I loved the feel of his body on mine, loved the roughness of his chest hair against my nipples and the feel of his cock softening inside of me. I made myself release him when he stirred against me and ignored the sense of loss when he pulled out and rolled on to his back beside me.

I stared at the ceiling, wondering if he would object if I cuddled him. Probably. Fucking and cuddling were two different things and Aiden Wright didn't strike me as the cuddling type.

I turned away from him, pulling up the quilt and tucking my arm under the pillow as I curled into a ball. Aiden curled up behind me, molding his lean body against my curves and cupping one heavy breast, and I couldn't resist relaxing into his warm grip. I stared at the fire wondering uneasily if tomorrow morning would be a repeat of our previous night in the cabin. Despite what he had said earlier, despite his obvious desire, Aiden had realized his mistake once before and he would most likely do it again.

If he does, that's fine, I told myself grimly. I had wanted a no-commitment fling and that's exactly what I was getting. If it was only for tonight, well, I had at least a year's worth of masturbatory fantasies from Aiden tasting me. It would have to be enough.

He didn't taste you. He ate your pussy and you fucking loved it.

Tell me something I don't know.

I closed my eyes, ignoring my urge to stay awake the entire night and enjoy the feel of Aiden's hard body against mine. I was fairly certain that women who enjoyed casual hook-ups didn't stay awake all night memorizing the feel of their lover's body against their own.

Casual hook-up. I could do this. No problem. No fucking problem.

"Lina?" Aiden's breath stirred my hair.

"Hmm?"

"Merry Christmas."

"Merry Christmas, Aiden."

Chapter 10

When I woke the next morning, the fire was low and the space behind me was empty. I touched the spot where Aiden's body had been before sighing loudly.

It doesn't matter, I told myself angrily. Stop being such a damn baby. I stared at King snoring loudly next to the fireplace before sitting up. I would have a hot shower and wait for Aiden to appear and tell me it was a mistake and –

"Good morning, Lina."

His low voice made me jump and I twisted to see him sitting on the couch behind me. I swallowed heavily. He was naked and his cock was fully erect. He was stroking it almost lazily with one hand and I licked my lips when a clear drop of liquid appeared at the top. He rubbed his thumb through it before smiling at me.

"Come here, princess."

I tugged the quilt around me and Aiden shook his head. "You don't need that."

My limbs trembling, I dropped the quilt and crawled across the mattress toward him. Aiden's eyes darkened with lust as he watched the way my heavy breasts swayed.

"Fuck," he muttered under his breath as I knelt between his legs and stared up at him.

He pushed his thumb into my mouth and I sucked at it eagerly, cleaning away his precum as I held his gaze.

He muttered another curse before cupping the back of my head and guiding it toward the head of his cock. I opened my mouth and sucked eagerly at his thick cock, sliding my tongue along the vein on the underside before swirling the tip of my tongue across the head. He sucked in his breath and gathered my hair into a ponytail.

"Suck harder," he demanded in a low voice.

I obeyed, sucking until my cheeks hollowed, and feeling a flush of pleasure when he crooned, "Such a good girl."

I wrapped my hand around the base of his cock, stroking firmly as I sucked and licked. His hips were rising to meet my mouth and I pulled back a little when the head of his cock pushed against the back of my throat.

I licked his cock and gave him an apologetic look. "I'm sorry."

He petted my hair and leaned back against the couch cushions. "You're doing very well, kitten. You don't have to be sorry."

I stroked his cock with my hand and he groaned lightly. "Suck, princess. Suck my cock."

I lowered my mouth over his dick and sucked enthusiastically as he thrust into my mouth.

"You're going to suck my dick until I come in your mouth," he said. "You're going to swallow it all, princess."

A snippet of my fantasy came back to me and my nipples tightened as liquid dripped from my pussy and slid down my inner thigh.

"If you don't," he rasped, "if one drop falls from that perfect, hot mouth, I'll spank you. Do you understand?"

I nodded around his cock and he tugged on my hair until his cock popped free from my mouth.

I licked at my swollen lips as he stared expectantly at me. "Yes, Aiden, I understand."

"Good," he said before gently pushing me back to his cock. "Now use your perfect, hot mouth to make me come."

I slid his cock past my lips and sucked like a woman possessed. I was determined to please Aiden and I used every trick my, admittedly limited experience, could come up with. Within less than five minutes, he was groaning loudly, his hips pumping back and forth as he worked his cock between my lips. It might have been my enthusiasm or maybe he had been jerking off for a while before I woke up but I didn't care. I wanted to taste him on my tongue and when his cock swelled in my mouth and he came with a hoarse shout, I sucked eagerly, taking everything he had to offer.

When he was finished, he gently pulled me upright and examined my flushed cheeks and swollen mouth. I smiled at him, licking my lips and rubbing his naked thighs with my hands as his gaze dropped to my breasts. An excited and self-satisfied look crossed his face and I looked down, my eyes widening at the drop of his come that rested on the swell of my right breast.

I lifted my gaze to Aiden and my thighs quivered when he said, "Naughty girl."

"Aiden – "

"You promised to swallow all of it, didn't you, princess?"

"Yes, Aiden."

"Did you?"

I swallowed as my stomach clenched with need and my pelvis began to throb. "No."

"My lap, kitten. Now."

I suppose I should have at least pretended to hesitate, my pride was screaming at me to, but my body was scrambling into position across his lap without a hint of shame. I had never been in this position before but I draped myself across his lap like an old pro. I pressed my face into the couch cushions, his hard thighs digging into my rib cage and one big hand resting lightly on the small of my back.

"It was only a drop, so I think ten will suffice, don't you, Ms. Jones?" Aiden asked.

My hands were already gripping the arm of the couch in anticipation and I nodded as Aiden's hand smoothed over the curve of my ass.

"Answer me, Ms. Jones."

"Yes, Aiden. Ten."

"Ask me nicely."

"Please, Aiden. Please will you spank me?"

Oh I liked this game. I liked it very much if my dripping pussy was any indication. I squirmed a little against his thighs and he squeezed my ass.

"Don't move, princess."

"Yes, Aiden," I said breathlessly.

"I want you to count."

"Yes, Aiden," I said again.

The first slap of his hand against my ass was a tingling sting of pleasure and pain.

"One," I cried.

"Very good, Ms. Jones."

I counted off the next nine slaps, my cries growing louder with each one. By the time he was finished, I was squirming and moaning and his cock was erect again and rubbing against the swell of my stomach.

"Such a good girl," he said and I felt a rush of pride at his pleased tone.

He rubbed my painful ass before tugging on my hair. "Ride me, Ms. Jones."

I straddled him, my knees digging into the couch cushions, and rubbed my wet pussy against his cock. He grinned at me as his hand fisted in my hair. "Someone's very wet, isn't she?"

I nodded as he reached between us and guided his cock into my pussy. I took him easily, my pussy clinging tightly to him as I pushed down until he was fully sheathed.

"Oh," I whispered. "It feels so good, Aiden."

"Move," he demanded hoarsely. "Hard and fast."

I did what he asked, rocking roughly against him as he thrust his hips up and down. His hands gripped my aching ass and he pushed me up and down, forcing me to meet each of his thrusts with an intensity that made me moan in pleasure.

"Touch yourself," he said. "I want you to come all over my cock."

I brushed my fingers over my clit as I held on to Aiden's shoulder with my other. I was panting, moaning, my hair was sticking to my sweaty face and I knew my breasts and belly were bouncing with every hard thrust of Aiden's cock. I didn't care. I wanted my release, wanted it badly, and I rubbed furiously at my clit until, with a sharp cry, I climaxed around Aiden's cock. He cursed then shouted my name as he pumped frantically into me and came with another hoarse shout. I collapsed against his broad chest, listening to his pounding heart beat beneath my cheek as he brushed the tips of his fingers over my back.

"Fuck, Lina," he muttered. "I'm going to spank you every goddamn day if it makes you come like that. Your pussy was like a fucking vice around my dick."

I laughed. "That's so sweet, Aiden."

We sat silently for a few moments before Aiden kissed the top of my head. "We should shower and go to Joe's. It's getting late and Steph always does a big Christmas breakfast."

I slid off his lap and wrapped the quilt around me. Bright sunlight was streaming through the windows and I was suddenly feeling self-conscious about my nudity. God, did every part of my body have to jiggle?

"I'll go first," I said brightly as Aiden frowned.

"Lina, you don't need to cover – "

I hurried into the bathroom before he could finish.

* * *

"Are you and Aiden dating?"

I finished placing the extra glassware in the china cabinet and closed the door before smiling at Susan. We were alone in the spare room but I could hear the voices of the other women in the kitchen and the lower, deeper pitch of the men in the living room.

"Well, are you?" Susan asked impatiently.

"No," I replied.

"I didn't think so. You're so not his type," she replied.

"No, I probably am not," I agreed cheerfully.

"Oh, you're not," she said again. "I've known Aiden for a lot of years and there are two things you need to know about him. One – he doesn't do relationships and two - the women he casually dates are always..."

She trailed off and I smiled at her. "Less fat?"

"Less curvy," she said firmly.

"If he doesn't do relationships, why are you so interested in him? I asked. "You don't strike me as the type of girl who would be happy with the casual hook-up."

"Oh, I'm going to change his mind," she said confidently. "Can I give you some advice?"

"Sure."

"You really shouldn't moon over Aiden the way you do. It's embarrassing for you and uncomfortable for Aiden."

I laughed out loud and Susan frowned at me. "What's so funny?"

She's young, I reminded myself. *She's young and has a crush on Aiden and she's the daughter of two people you happen to like very much. Don't be cruel to her.*

"Nothing," I said. "Thank you for the advice."

She nodded before glancing at the open doorway and lowering her voice. "Listen, I'm going to stay with Aiden tonight. I need you to tell my mother that you're perfectly happy with staying here and would prefer it."

She gave me a dreamy little smile. "I've been waiting years for this opportunity and tonight Aiden's finally going to realize I'm not a little girl anymore."

"Is that why you think he's not with you?" I asked.

"What else would it be?" She asked. "I mean, look at me."

The girl had confidence, I had to give her that, and I was a fool if I didn't admit that I envied that confidence, just a little.

"He wants me," she said happily. "I've seen the way he watches me when he thinks I'm not looking. Why should I make him deny his attraction any longer?"

I didn't reply and she smiled again at me. "Listen, Lina. I'm sure you're a lovely person and, trust me, I know what it's like to have a crush on someone. But someone like you doesn't have a chance with someone like Aiden and you know what the right thing to do is. Let me have my night with Aiden. I'm going to rock his world."

Her condescending tone set my teeth on edge and, my body shaking with sudden anger, I said sweetly, "I'm sorry, Susan. I can't do that."

"Of course you can," she said. "Just tell my mother that – "

"I really can't," I interrupted. "Aiden and I aren't dating but we are fucking and I have Aiden's 'world rocking' firmly under control."

Susan's mouth dropped open and I smiled again at her before pushing past her and walking out of the room. Almost immediately my feeling of triumph dissipated and I was left feeling ill and ashamed. I had deliberately hurt her to make myself feel better and for what? Aiden and I had no future past the holidays. He wasn't interested in Susan but I hadn't needed to be so cruel to her. Aiden didn't belong to me and rubbing our temporary, sex-only arrangement in a young girl's face made me an awful person. Feeling sick to my stomach, I turned around. I needed to apologize to Susan.

"Lina? Are you ready to go?"

Aiden's deep voice spoke quietly behind me as Susan slipped out from the spare room. She glared angrily at me before lifting her gaze to Aiden.

"Susan? What's wrong?" Aiden asked.

"Nothing," she spat. "Leave me alone, Aiden."

She stomped away as Aiden glanced at me curiously. "What was that about?"

I sighed. "Can we go back to your cabin? I'm suddenly very tired."

* * *

"Lina, will you tell me what's wrong?" Aiden asked quietly.

I was sitting on the far end of the couch, King's giant head in my lap, and staring silently into the fire. Aiden was sitting at the opposite end and I had been trying my best to ignore my urge to slide over and cuddle against him.

Not that type of relationship, I reminded myself.

"I told Susan we were fucking," I confessed. "I'm sorry."

"That explains why she was so angry," he said.

"I shouldn't have told her and I'm really sorry," I said again.

"You don't have to apologize. In fact, it might make my life a little easier," Aiden said. "Not that I'm exactly proud of making you do my dirty work for me but the situation with Susan was starting to get out of control."

I glanced at him and he gave me a small smile of embarrassment. "Joe's my best friend and I was worried about offending him by rejecting his daughter."

"It's only a temporary solution," I said. "Susan knows we're not dating, only fucking, so as soon as you're here alone, I imagine she'll be all over you again. You really need to man up and tell her you'll never be interested – preferably before she goes back to London."

He nodded. "You're right."

I stared suspiciously at him. "Why are you being so agreeable to everything I say?"

"Maybe because I finally realized you're always right?"

That made me laugh and Aiden smiled happily at me as I said, "I'm going to assume that attitude will carry over to the work place?"

He just shrugged and I rolled my eyes before petting King's head. "I had my hopes up for a moment there."

He laughed quietly and I grinned at him as he slid across the couch and rested his hand on my thigh. King licked at his hand and he gently petted the big dog. "Are you going to go out with Parker?"

"What?" I blinked at the sudden change in topic.

"Are you going to start dating Parker after the holidays?" He asked. "He wants you, Lina. You know he does."

"I don't know," I said. "I hadn't really thought about it."

"He's a player," Aiden said. His hand tightened on my thigh for a moment. "You should stay away from him."

"You don't know he's a player," I replied. "You know nothing about him outside of work."

"I know men like him," Aiden said. "He'll say and do all the right things to get you into bed and once he's bored, he'll move on. It's nothing but sex to him."

I laughed and Aiden flushed brightly. "I'm not like him, Lina. I'm always honest with a woman about what I want and what I can give them before I sleep with them. The only time I've fucked that up was that night I was stranded here with you. I should have been clear with you about what I wanted before I slept with you and I wasn't. But, in my defense, I had wanted you for three years and to finally have you in my bed..."

He trailed off and gave me a rueful look. "I temporarily lost my damn mind."

I smiled faintly. "Resulting in an extremely awkward next morning. I bet you'll never do that again."

"I'm sorry, Lina. I shouldn't have – "

"It's fine," I interrupted. "You don't need to keep apologizing for it."

"Lina, I – "

"Why don't you do relationships?" I asked.

He didn't reply and I grimaced. "Sorry, I'm being nosy."

He stared into the fire and I twitched with surprise when he said, "When I was fifteen, my father cheated on my mother."

I patted his leg gingerly. "I'm sorry. You don't have to tell me this."

To my surprise, he continued. "My mother was, understandably, devastated and they separated for over a year. It was awful to watch her go through the pain of what he had done. My father was remorseful and begged for her forgiveness. I guess they were going through a rough patch and he made a stupid mistake."

He smiled bitterly at me. "One stupid mistake that destroyed my mother. They did counselling separately and together and eventually my mother forgave him and my dad moved back in. As far as I know, he's never cheated again but..."

He stopped and stared at King's head. "My mom was never the same after that. Either was my dad. They love each other, at least I think they do, but she doesn't trust him and I don't think she ever will. And my dad is still being eaten alive by his guilt. To others they seem to have the perfect relationship but I actually think they would have been better off to go their separate ways."

He sighed and glanced quickly at me. "To see their relationship go from one that was damn near perfect to how it is now? I don't want to ever go through that."

"Just because your father made a mistake and cheated on your mother, doesn't mean you will," I said cautiously. "You shouldn't deny yourself the chance at happiness, at love, on the assumption that you'll make the same mistakes. You're not your father."

"Maybe not," he replied. "But how many couples do you know who are truly happy?"

"Joe and Steph are happy," I said. "My parents are happy."

"You don't know that for certain," he said.

"No, I suppose I don't. But no relationship is perfect. They have their ups and downs and they require commitment and effort once the novelty wears off. People make mistakes, Aiden. It's just human nature."

"My parents have been secretly miserable for years and just refuse to admit it," Aiden said.

"They've chosen to be that way. You can choose something different," I said.

"I have," he replied quietly.

"But does that make you happy?"

"Yes," he said. "It does."

"Then I guess that's all that matters," I replied.

We sat in silence for a few moments. I kept a neutral look on my face but inwardly my heart was breaking for Aiden.

Just Aiden? Or do you feel sorry for you, as well?

Yes, I decided, I felt sorry for me too. I had agreed to a casual fling over the holidays with Aiden, hell, I had pushed him for it, but there had been a small part of me that hoped he wanted more. Aiden's confession and his quick affirmation that he was happy without the entanglement of a relationship had killed that small, hopeful part of me and I mourned its loss.

Get over it, girl. You wanted this, remember?

"Do you want me to walk you back over to Joe's place?" Aiden asked suddenly.

I shook my head no before pushing King's head from my lap and straddling Aiden's. I pressed my mouth against his neck and rubbed his broad shoulders. "Of course not. Unless you don't want me here."

"You know I do," he said.

"Then it's all good," I said.

"Is it?" He cupped the back of my neck and tugged my face up.

"Yes."

"Are you sure you're happy with this," he paused, "arrangement?"

"I am," I said.

"Lina – "

"Aiden, stop," I said. "I'm good, okay? We only have two more days of holidays left. Let's just enjoy it."

"I do want you, Lina. Very much," he said.

"Good," I replied. "Now stop talking and show me."

* * *

"Let me get this straight." Tracy swept aside the crinkled Christmas paper and folded her hands on top of the table. "You spent the holidays having a sex-filled fling with your hottie of a boss who you hate."

I laughed and nodded. "Yes. I love this necklace, by the way. Thank you."

"Who cares about Christmas presents," Tracy said. "You're fucking your boss!"

"I was fucking my boss," I corrected. "Now I'm not."

"Lina," Tracy gave me an earnest look, "what's happening to you? I was gone to Panama for six weeks and I come back to find you hooking up with a guy you find hot but absolutely hate."

"I don't hate him," I said. "And I always lusted after him – you know that."

"Yeah, I know but you said he didn't want you."

"I was wrong," I said. "Pleasantly so."

"Then why aren't you dating?"

"I told you – he doesn't do relationships."

"And now suddenly you don't either?" Tracy gave me a skeptical look.

I shrugged nonchalantly. "I wanted to try an experiment and I did."

"An experiment," Tracy said. "You're telling me that you wanted to find out if you're the type of person who can just sleep with someone without it meaning anything."

"Yes."

Tracy took my hand and squeezed it. "Honey, you didn't need an experiment for that. You and I both know you're not."

I pulled my hand free with a scowl. "We didn't know that. And besides, I actually think I am."

"Honey, you're not," Tracy said gently.

"If I wasn't, would I be considering asking him if he wanted to keep going?"

Tracy's eyes widened. "Lina, you aren't."

"I am," I said with feigned disinterest. "The sex was amazing and I miss it."

Missing sex with Aiden was the understatement of the year. It had been two days since we had left the cabin and I had thought of nothing but sex with Aiden. I was going back to work tomorrow and I was already wondering how I would make it through the day without throwing myself at him. Last night, lying sleepless in my bed, the answer had hit me. I would ask Aiden if he wanted to keep having sex. There was no harm in it. We both knew what it was and once I had gotten this need out of my system, I would end it.

And if he already has? If he says 'thanks but no thanks', then what?

Then I would be a goddamn adult and accept it.

"Lina, you're playing a dangerous game," Tracy said. "Sex without feelings, without commitment, isn't your thing."

"Why can't it be?" I asked her. "I was in a relationship for four years and I got nothing from it but a broken heart and a belief that I suck in bed. Aiden makes me feel good, Tracy. He makes me feel sexy and beautiful and – "

"You can find that with someone else," Tracy interrupted. "Someone who isn't your boss and who wants more than a roll in the hay. Someone who isn't going to break your heart."

"My heart is perfectly fine," I said briskly. "Stop worrying, Tracy."

"Someone has to," she said. "You've gone off the deep end."

I laughed. "No, I haven't. I'm just having some fun for the first time in my life. Let me live a little, will you?"

"This is going to end so badly," Tracy said morosely.

"It won't," I assured her. "I know what I'm doing."

* * *

Late Monday morning I knocked on Aiden's office door. At his gruff 'come in', I stepped into the room and shut the door firmly behind me. My heart was racing from nervousness but I was determined to talk to Aiden about continuing our fling. I wanted him badly and I didn't care what Tracy said – I could have a casual hook-up, no problem.

"Good morning, Aiden. How was your weekend?" I asked.

"Fine, Ms. Jones. How was yours?" He replied without looking up from his computer.

My resolve faltered at the coldness of his tone and I cleared my throat nervously. "It was good, thank you."

He continued to stare silently at his computer screen as I weighed my options. Maybe he was having a bad morning and it had nothing to do with me. He had been holed up in his office since I arrived and I knew he was busy.

"What can I help you with, Ms. Jones?" He finally asked.

"Uh, I emailed you the Robins document," I said.

"I received it, thank you."

I continued to hesitate in his doorway and he finally glanced at me. "Is there something else?"

I gathered my courage. "Yes. Aiden, I wondered if you wanted to – "

His cell phone buzzed and he held up his hand toward me. "I need to take this."

I nodded and he raised one eyebrow before glancing at the door.

"Right, I'll, um, just go. Sorry," I stammered before slipping out of his office.

Well, fuck. Aiden was finished with me. I sat down in my chair and stared blankly at the computer screen.

No big deal, Lina, I told myself fiercely. *You knew asking him to keep going was a long shot, hell, it was more than a long shot. It would have been a damn miracle if he had wanted to keep fucking you. You fucked like bunnies over the holidays and just because it wasn't enough for you, doesn't mean it was the same for him.*

I pulled a file toward me and took a deep breath. I could do this. I was the queen of the casual fling. Aiden's rejection didn't bother me – not in the least.

Chapter 11

"Hello, gorgeous. How were your holidays?" Jamie dropped into the seat next to me. "Mind if I share your table? It's busy in here today."

I looked around the crowded café. "I think everyone's waiting until after New Years' to start their healthy eating habits."

He laughed. "I think you're right. So, how was your Christmas?"

"It was good. How was yours?" I asked before biting into my sandwich.

"Quiet. Good though. Better than your boss' anyway."

"What do you mean?" I asked.

Jamie laughed. "You can't tell me that you haven't noticed the horrible mood he's been in this morning. You're his assistant, for God's sake."

I made myself smile at him. "He does seem pretty grumpy. I think he's just really busy. We have a bunch of work to finish before the end of the year. I have a feeling I'll be earning some overtime this week."

"Lucky you," Jamie said with a grin. "I don't suppose you could find some time to have dinner with me this week?"

"Jamie, I don't think – "

"Mind if I join you?"

I blinked in surprise when Aiden sat down next to me. He had a bowl of soup and a water and he crumbled some crackers into his soup as Jamie frowned at him. "What are you doing here?"

"Good to see you too, Parker," Aiden said mildly. "And I'm having lunch. Enjoy your holidays?"

"Yes, thanks," Jamie said before glancing at me.

I took another bite of my sandwich. The café table was small and I could feel Aiden's thigh brushing against mine. I cleared my throat and reached for my unopened bottle of water. The cap was stupidly tight and after watching me fumble uselessly at it for a few seconds, Aiden took the bottle of water and twisted off the cap.

"Thank you, Mr. Wright."

"You're welcome, Ms. Jones," he said politely. I gave Jamie a nervous smile as Aiden ate silently.

"So are you busy tonight, Lina?" Jamie asked. Apparently he had decided ignoring Aiden's presence was the best option. "Do you want to have dinner?"

"I need Ms. Jones to work late tonight," Aiden said immediately.

"How late?" I asked. "I have plans."

"What plans?" Aiden frowned at me and Jamie snorted.

"That's not really any of your business, Aiden."

"What are you doing tonight?" Aiden ignored him completely.

"I'm going to the animal shelter to look at dogs," I said.

Aiden relaxed in his chair as Jamie smiled at me. "You like dogs?"

"I do," I said. "My dog passed away before the holidays and my house is too empty without a dog."

"I'm really sorry for your loss," Jamie picked up my hand and squeezed it tightly before brushing his thumb across my knuckles. I jumped when Aiden's spoon clattered to the table and gave him a quick glance. He was glaring daggers at Jamie and the CFO was staring coolly at him.

"Something wrong, Aiden?"

Aiden continued to glare at him and I kicked his shin under the table. His gaze snapped to me and his nostrils flared angrily before he shoved his half-eaten bowl of soup away and snatched up his water bottle.

"Lina? Why don't I take you for dinner first and then go with you to the shelter? I can help you pick out the perfect dog," Jamie said.

"I still need you to work late," Aiden reminded me.

"Jesus, Aiden. Have a heart for once. Her dog just died."

"I'm well aware of that, Parker," Aiden snapped. "But I still need her to do her job."

"Seriously? You can't even – "

"It's fine," I interrupted. "I can go to the shelter another night."

"Lina," Jamie said, "you shouldn't have to – "

"It's fine," I repeated before pulling my hand free of Jamie's grip and glancing at my watch. "If you'll excuse me, I'm going to head back to the office."

"I'll walk with you," Jamie said. He stood and offered me his arm and, forcing myself not to glance at Aiden, I hooked my hand around Jamie's arm and followed him out of the café.

* * *

"Trying to make me jealous isn't going to work, Ms. Jones."

I glanced up from the photocopier. Aiden was leaning in the doorway of the copy room and I smiled briefly at him before feeding more paper into the top tray.

"Good to know."

"I mean it," he said. "I'm not the jealous type and even if I were, a casual hook-up with someone doesn't warrant jealousy."

"Thanks for clearing that up," I said before punching the copier buttons a little harder than necessary.

"It's a waste of time trying to make me jealous," he said.

"I heard you the first time," I said.

"As long as we're perfectly clear that there's no point in using Parker to try and – "

"I'm not using Jamie Parker to do anything," I interrupted. "And while we're on the subject of Jamie – making me stay late and work on bogus files to keep me away from him isn't going to work either."

"I have no idea what you're talking about," Aiden said stiffly.

"I'm sure you don't," I said. I picked up the stack of copied papers and handed them to him. "Here's the last of what you needed. I'm going to head home unless you have another file that just has to be finished for tomorrow?"

He didn't reply and I smiled sweetly at him. "Have a good evening, Mr. Wright."

* * *

"So, dinner tonight and then the animal shelter?" Jamie leaned against my desk and smiled at me.

It was the next afternoon and while I wasn't deliberately avoiding Jamie, I hadn't been actively seeking him out either. I sighed inwardly and glanced at Aiden's door. He was out for a meeting for at least another half hour and I made a sudden decision.

"Jamie, will you walk to Starbucks with me? I need a coffee break."

He nodded. "Sure. Lead the way, gorgeous."

Ten minutes later, we were sitting in the Starbucks and I took a sip of coffee as Jamie said, "You asked me to coffee to tell me you're not the least bit interested in me, didn't you, Lina?"

I smiled faintly at him. "I'm sorry, Jamie."

He shrugged. "I can't say I'm not disappointed."

"I wish I was, truly. You're a great guy and – "

He laughed and held up his hand. "You don't have to say that, Lina."

"It's true," I insisted.

"Just out of curiosity, are you not interested in me because of Aiden Wright or because I'm not your type?"

I hesitated and Jamie sighed. "He's a player, Lina. He's attracted to you – that's obvious – but it will never be anything more than sex."

"He says the same thing about you."

"He doesn't even know me."

"And you don't know him," I said gently.

"So I'm wrong then?" Jamie asked. "He wants more from you than just sex?"

"No," I said. "You're not wrong."

He frowned at me and I fiddled with the lid of my coffee cup. "Is he wrong about you?"

"Well, I'm not going to deny that I really want to see you naked, but I don't know if that's all I want or not. I'm open to dating and seeing where it leads which is more than you're going to get from Aiden Wright."

I laughed. "Gee, that's so romantic, Jamie."

"If you're looking for romance, Aiden Wright is the wrong direction to look in."

"I know," I said. "But it doesn't feel right to date you when I want him."

"Okay then," Jamie said. "I'll stop bugging you to go out with me."

"I really am sorry, Jamie," I said.

"Don't worry about it. It's always better to be honest, don't you think?" He said.

"Yes."

"Good. Hey, what do you think my chances are with Amanda?"

"She has a girlfriend and they've been together for nearly seven years so I'd say zero."

"Damn," he muttered. "A guy can't catch a break. Oh well, there's always online dating."

I laughed and he grinned at me. "Listen, if you want someone to go with you to the shelter, my offer still stands. Strictly as friends, of course."

"That's nice of you but I'm fine to go alone," I said before glancing at my watch. "I'd better get back. It's busy and I need to finish a few files this afternoon if I don't want to stay late again."

When we were back in the office, Jamie lingered at my desk for a moment. "Thanks for the coffee and honesty, Lina."

"Thanks for understanding," I replied.

"If you ever change your mind, you know where to – "

"Ms. Jones!"

I twitched, spilling coffee on my hand, and turned to Aiden's office. He was standing in the doorway, glaring at Jamie and me and I smiled cheerfully at him.

"Yes, Mr. Wright?"

My office. Now." He turned on his heel and stalked into his office as I rolled my eyes at Jamie.

"Need me to stay and defend your honour?" Jamie asked.

I grinned. "No. I'm more than capable of handling Aiden Wright. Thanks again, Jamie."

As he walked away I set my coffee down and, preparing myself for battle, walked into Aiden's office.

"Shut the door," he barked.

I shut the door and stood where I was as Aiden sat on the edge of his desk and scowled at me.

"What can I do for you, Mr. Wright?"

"You can be at your desk when I need you," he snapped, "instead of disappearing with Parker. I'm not paying you to fuck him."

My mouth dropped open. "I am not fucking Jamie."

"Where did the two of you go?"

"None of your business," I said.

"You will tell me, Ms. Jones, or – "

"Or what? You'll spank me?" I stomped toward him. "That's over, remember?"

"I remember," he said tightly. "But I pay you to work for me, not disappear with the CFO to do God knows what."

"You know, Mr. Wright, for someone who says he doesn't get jealous, you're sounding awfully jealous."

"I am not jealous," he ground out.

"Please," I rolled my eyes, "you're practically green."

"Just tell me what you were doing with Parker," he said.

"Coffee," I said. "We went for coffee. I have coffee breath - did you want me to blow you so you have proof?"

A weird look crossed his face and my eyes widened as I realized exactly what I had just said.

"Blow ON you, I meant," I said quickly. "So you can smell the coffee. On my breath."

He didn't reply but there was a smug little grin on his face that made me want to punch him.

"Forget it," I muttered. I turned to walk away and Aiden grabbed my arm. He yanked me between his legs, one hand cupping my ass and pressing me against his growing erection and the other tangling in my hair.

"Aiden," I said unsteadily, "what are you doing?"

"Do you think I'm going to just let you walk away after you offer to blow me?" He said.

"That was an accident," I said. "A slip of the tongue only."

"Just thinking about your tongue on my dick makes me so fucking hard," he replied.

Heat rushed through me and, God help me, a gush of wetness that practically rendered my panties unwearable. I squirmed against him as he squeezed my ass again before unzipping the back of my skirt.

"The door is unlocked," I hissed at him as he slipped his hand inside my skirt. His eyes widened as he touched my naked ass cheeks and then the straps of my garter belt.

"Are you wearing a thong and garters?"

I stared at the wall over his shoulder. It had been ridiculous but yesterday and today I had dressed in the sexy lingerie I bought over the weekend. Since I was considering asking Aiden to continue on with our fling, it had seemed like a good idea to pick up a few pairs of sexy panties and matching garters. Of course, yesterday he had made it perfectly clear we were finished but it hadn't been enough to stop me from wearing them this morning.

The lust on his face was unmistakeable and I trembled as more liquid dripped from my pussy.

"Did you wear them for me or for Parker?" He asked hoarsely.

I didn't reply and his hard fingers bit into my ass. "Answer me, Ms. Jones."

"You," I whispered.

I squeaked in surprise when he suddenly pushed me away and slid off the desk. He crossed the room and locked the door before giving me a predatory grin that made me hotter than fucking fire.

"Aiden, what — what are you doing?" I said as he stalked toward me.

"I need to eat your pussy, Ms. Jones."

My eyes widened and I took a step back, my ass bumping against the edge of his desk. "Aiden, you can't. We're at work and it's not — "

His hands tugged my skirt around my waist and I slapped ineffectively at them. "Aiden, you can't!"

"Oh yes I fucking can," he growled before lifting me and sitting me on his desk. He pushed me down, I yelped when his stapler dug into the small of my back, and he yanked it out from under me before tossing it on the floor.

"Don't move, Ms. Jones."

"Aiden — "

"Don't move," he said again before pushing my thighs apart.

"Christ, you are so fucking hot," he muttered to himself as his hands traced the edge of my stockings.

"Aiden, this really isn't appropriate," I moaned as he bent his head and pressed his nose against the wet fabric of my panties. He inhaled deeply before licking me though the fabric.

"I've missed your pussy," he muttered again. His fingers curled into the waistband of my panties and I gasped loudly when he tore them apart.

"I just bought those!"

"I'll buy you more," he said, stuffing my panties into his pocket. The air was cool against my throbbing pussy and I pressed my thighs against his hips.

"Aiden, we need to – "

My plea for him to stop ended the moment he licked my pussy. My hands buried themselves in his hair and I pushed his face against my hot core. His hands slipped under my ass, kneading the flesh as he lifted me slightly and slid his tongue inside of me.

"Oh fuck," I whispered. "Oh fuck, Aiden."

"Have you missed this, kitten?" He raised his head, my juices gleaming on his mouth and chin, and grinned at me. "Have you missed having my tongue in your pussy?"

"Yes!" I whispered. "God, yes. Don't stop."

He licked the lips of my pussy clean before raising his head again. "Are you going to let Parker do this to you?"

I blinked at him, my hands tightening in his hair. "Seriously? Aiden, stop talking about the fucking CFO and eat my pussy!" I said in a loud whisper.

"Your pussy belongs to me," he said. "Tell me you won't let Parker anywhere near it."

"I won't!" I snapped at him. "For God's sake, Aiden!"

"Say it belongs to me," he said calmly.

"You! It belongs to you!" I was almost desperate for relief and I pulled so sharply on his hair that he muttered a low curse.

"It's my pussy," he said again, "and no one is allowed to touch it, eat it or fuck it but me."

He dipped his head and licked and nibbled at my wet lips before thrusting his tongue between them to lick my clit. I threw my arm over my mouth to muffle my moans of pleasure and rocked my hips against his face.

He lifted his head again and I whimpered with need and disappointment.

"Promise me, princess. Promise you won't let anyone eat or fuck your pussy but me," he demanded.

I was so fucking close that I would have promised him my first-born child if it meant he would bury his head between my thighs again. "I promise. No one but you, Aiden. I promise."

He rewarded my breathless agreement by pushing his face into my pussy and sucking greedily at my clit. I came immediately, my hips thrusting helplessly and my loud shriek of pleasure dampened by my arm. I moaned and thrust and shuddered as Aiden licked me clean. I nearly fell off the desk when our receptionist's voice came over the intercom on the phone next to my head.

"Mr. Wright? Your four o'clock is here."

Aiden lifted his head from my dripping pussy. "Put him in the boardroom please. I'll be there in five minutes."

"Shit," I whispered as Aiden helped me into a sitting position. "Your face is..."

I trailed off as my cheeks flamed red.

Aiden grinned at me. "Covered in your sweet juices?"

"Oh God," I said. "What the hell did we just do?"

He grinned smugly at me. "I just made you come all over my face. Have you forgotten? Do I need to do it again?"

I tugged my skirt down. "You have a meeting with a client!" I hissed at him. "Your face and, oh God, your tie and your shirt are wet!"

He tugged off his tie and unbuttoned his shirt. "I always keep an extra set of clothes at the office."

I followed him into his private bathroom and watched as he washed his face and hands before unzipping the suit bag that was hanging on the back of the door.

"Why do you keep extra clothes here?" I asked. "Exactly how many pussies have you eaten in your office?"

He laughed so loudly that I made a shushing gesture with my hands.

"Truthfully? Yours is the only one," he said as he shrugged into his shirt. "I tend to keep my personal life separate from my work life. Of course," he eyed my dark nylons, "that was before I knew you were wearing garters to the office just for me."

"I wore them for me," I said.

"That's not what you said earlier," he said cheerfully. His bad mood had disappeared completely.

"I was lying," I said.

"Because you want me to spank you?" He arched his eyebrow at me and I shook my head.

"No, of course not."

He kissed me deeply and, God help me, the taste of my own essence that still lingered on his lips made me instantly wet again.

"Aiden," I whispered when he released my mouth. "I want to be with you."

He stared cautiously at me. "Lina, I thought I made it clear that - "

"Yes, I know," I said grouchily. "Jesus, Aiden, I'm not asking you to marry me. I want to keep having sex with you. No dating, no commitment, just sex, okay?"

"You don't want that," he said.

"Um, yes I do," I argued. "And you want it too – admit it."

He slipped into his fresh shirt. "Obviously I want that but you're not the type of woman to have a casual affair with someone."

"You don't know that."

"You told me you weren't into it," he said as he tucked his shirt into his pants and reached for his tie. "At the cabin."

"I've changed my mind," I said.

"Just like that?"

"Just like that," I said. "I'm offering you exactly what you want. No commitment, no flowers or romance, just good old fashioned fucking. How long do your flings usually last?"

He gave me an uncomfortable look and I grabbed his tie and handed it to him. "How long, Aiden?"

"About a month," he muttered before facing the mirror and tying his tie.

"Okay, we have a month to get this out of our system. After that, we end it – no drama."

"What about Parker?"

"What about him?"

"If you're sleeping with me, I don't want you dating him or anyone else. I'm not good at sharing."

"I hadn't noticed," I said sarcastically. "Don't worry about Jamie. I won't be dating him."

"Why not?"

I laughed. "That's none of your business."

I helped him into his suit jacket and smoothed it across his broad shoulders. "C'mon, cowboy. I won't ask again. Are you in or are you out?"

"I'm in," he said before giving me a hesitant look. "Lina, are you sure about this?"

"Yes," I said firmly. "Text me your address and I'll come by your place tonight. If you don't have plans?"

"I don't," he said. "Why don't you come for dinner? I'll order in and – "

"I can't," I said. "I have dinner plans. But I'll come by after. Say around nine?"

He frowned before nodding. "I'll see you then."

"Good," I said cheerfully. "Do you mind if I use your bathroom to freshen up?"

He shook his head and I herded him out of the room. "See you at nine, Aiden."

I closed the door and stared at myself in the mirror before gripping the sink tightly. What the hell was I doing?

You're getting what you want.

Yeah, for a damn month. Do you really think you can sleep with Aiden for a month and then just walk away? Go to work every day after that knowing that he had his fill of you and moved on to someone else?

Yes, I decided. I could. Besides, I didn't have a choice. I wanted Aiden and this was the only way to have him. It would have to be enough. I had lied about having dinner plans, but if I was going to protect my heart I needed to be careful. I couldn't get emotional or start pretending Aiden wanted more, and even that simple dinner invitation had been enough to start a spark of hope.

Nope, don't do that to yourself, Lina. Remember what this is.

I stared grimly at my reflection. Yes, I would need to be extremely careful to always remember what this was.

* * *

"Wow, your place is amazing." I stared out the large window at the sparkling lights of the city spread out below us. "I suppose I shouldn't be surprised that you live in a penthouse downtown, but I kind of am. The cabin is so rustic and this is…"

I trailed off and Aiden raised his eyebrows at me. "This is what?"

"Very luxurious," I said.

He laughed and handed me a glass of wine. "I worked hard to get where I am and I like to enjoy it."

"How rich are you, anyway?" I asked as I sipped at my wine. "Are you Mark Zuckerberg rich?"

He snorted laughter again before shaking his head. "Not even close."

I grinned at him and took another sip of wine. "This is delicious. Thank you."

"You're welcome. Are you hungry? I'm not much of a cook but I have cheese and crackers and – "

"Nope, I'm good," I said. "Why don't you give me a tour of your fancy penthouse? I'm assuming you provide a complimentary map so I can find my way to the front door after we're finished?"

Small frown lines appeared between his eyes. "Follow me, Ms. Jones."

He reached for my hand and I tucked them into my pockets before smiling at him. "Lead the way, Mr. Wright."

Ten minutes later we were standing in his bedroom and I studied the king-sized bed as a trickle of lust went through me. "You have a really lovely home, Aiden."

"Thank you."

"But four bathrooms? Really? You live alone and you have four bathrooms," I teased gently.

"Five actually." He opened the door to our left and I stuck my head into the master bathroom.

"Holy shit," I breathed. "Your bathroom is bigger than my bedroom. Are those multiple showerheads?"

He nodded and I grinned at him. "Very nice. I'll admit I'm jealous. My shower only has one showerhead and half the time it produces nothing more than a trickle of water. I bought a new showerhead for it but couldn't figure out how to replace it. I really need to Youtube it."

I smoothed my hand across the marble countertop before studying the giant bathtub in the corner. "You could go swimming in that thing."

"You can use it anytime you want," he said.

"Thanks. I might take you up on that one day," I said before following him out of the bathroom.

"Do you want more wine?" He pointed to my empty wine glass and I shook my head before setting it on top of the dresser.

"No, thank you."

I pulled my t-shirt over my head and dropped it on the floor. Aiden stared silently at me and I hesitated at the button of my jeans.

"Is something wrong, Aiden?"

"No," he said. "You just – "

"I just what?" I asked when he paused.

"You seem different."

"Do I?" I unbuttoned my jeans and tugged them down before stepping out of them. "What do you think of my new lingerie?"

Aiden studied my dark red bra and panty set. "I like it very much," he said hoarsely.

I smiled happily and tugged at the bottom of his shirt. "Raise your arms."

He did what I asked and I pulled off his shirt before tracing my hand across his abdomen to the button on his jeans. He watched silently as I unbuttoned them and shoved them down his hips. He was naked underneath them and I smiled my approval when his cock sprang free. He was already half-erect and he made a soft moan when I dropped to my knees in front of him and took his cock into my mouth. I sucked lightly on the head as his hands tangled in my hair.

"So good," he muttered before urging me to take more of his cock.

I spent nearly fifteen minutes on my knees in front of him, silently thankful for the thick carpet that cushioned my knees and shins, until Aiden was moaning loudly and thrusting his hips rapidly back and forth.

I released him and stroked his hard shaft with my hand as I tried to think of a graceful way to stand. Before I could formulate a solid plan, Aiden's hands were hooking into my armpits and he lifted me to my feet.

"My bed, Lina. Now," he rasped.

I smiled seductively and traced one finger down his chest. "Whatever you say, Aiden."

"Fuck," he muttered. He turned me around roughly and quickly unclasped my bra before tugging it free. He cupped my large breasts, pinching and tugging on my nipples until they were hard points, and kissing the back of my shoulder.

He led me to the bed and eased my panties down my legs. "You owe me a pair of panties," I reminded him as I scooted on to the bed.

He grinned and tossed my panties on the floor before pushing his way between my thighs. "I remember."

His cock was at my wet entrance and pushing its way in before I knew what was happening. I moaned, my legs clinging to his hips as he moved in an easy slide and retreat rhythm.

"Touch your clit, princess," he groaned. "I want to feel you come."

I reached between us and rubbed delicately at my clit as Aiden's rhythm turned deeper and harder. I moaned my approval and cupped my breast, pulling at my nipple until Aiden dipped his head and sucked it into his mouth. I clutched at his dark head, my hips rising to meet each of his thrusts as I circled my clit with the tips of my fingers.

Aiden lifted his head and pressed a kiss against my mouth. "I've missed you, Lina."

"I've missed fucking you too," I said.

Those little frown lines reappeared between his eyes and I smoothed them away with my finger. "What's wrong?"

"Nothing," he said.

I smiled at him and kissed him lightly. "You're slowing down. Don't slow down, please."

He returned my kiss and I groaned into his mouth as he fucked me roughly.

"Yes, just like that," I panted. The pleasure was building in my body and I rubbed faster, tugging lightly at my clit as I closed my eyes.

"Lina, look at me," Aiden demanded.

I ignored him, keeping my eyes shut tightly as I climaxed wildly. Above me, Aiden cursed loudly and his thrusting first slowed then quickened. My pussy squeezed him rhythmically as my orgasm flowed through me and I made a cat-like grin of satisfaction when he shouted hoarsely and I felt warm wetness flood my pussy. He shuddered above me and I pressed a kiss against his bare shoulder before opening my eyes.

Aiden, panting harshly, was staring at me and I stroked my fingers across his cheek. "You're getting kind of heavy, handsome."

He rolled off of me and I curled up against him, resting my head against his chest as he stroked my bare back. I enjoyed fifteen minutes of cuddling, fifteen minutes of savouring the warmth of Aiden's skin and listening to the steady beat of his heart, before I sat up.

"What's wrong?" Aiden asked.

"Nothing's wrong."

I slid out of the bed and tugged on my panties before reaching for my bra.

"Where are you going?"

"Home," I said. I put on my bra and stepped into my jeans as Aiden sat up.

"I thought you would spend the night."

"I can't," I said. "It's late and I have work in the morning and my boss will be pissed if I'm late."

He ignored my teasing and scowled at me. "You don't have to leave, Lina."

"I know," I replied cheerfully before slipping my shirt over my head. I leaned over the bed and kissed him briefly.

"I want you to stay," he said.

"That's sweet but I really can't. I'll sleep better in my own bed, and I didn't bring a change of clothes which means I'll have to get up super early if I stay the night. I'll see you tomorrow at the office, okay?"

I pressed another quick kiss against his mouth and then hurried to the door of his bedroom before he could argue. "I had fun tonight. Thanks, Aiden."

I shut his bedroom door and made my way through the dark to the elevator. I hit the button before yanking on my coat and my boots and grabbing my purse. I was half-convinced that Aiden would appear, demanding that I return to his bedroom and I wasn't sure if I was relieved or disappointed when the elevator doors slid open and Aiden hadn't appeared.

I rode the elevator down to the lobby, smoothing my 'just been fucked' hair into a ponytail, and nodded to the doorman before slipping into the night air. It was freezing out and I thought longingly of Aiden's warm body and bed before walking briskly to my car. I couldn't spend the night. I couldn't get used to sleeping in his bed or feeling his warm body against mine. It would just make things more difficult when our month was up.

* * *

"You know you don't always have to come to my place. I can go to your house," Aiden said.

It was Thursday night and I was lying in Aiden's bed. I had just been inwardly congratulating myself on how well I was doing at keeping things casual. Aiden had suggested dinner each night and I had graciously declined before suggesting I stop by later in the evening. And even though it had only been three nights, I figured I deserved some inner fist-bumping at the way I had left Aiden's bed immediately after we finished fucking and gone home to my lonely, cold bed. Especially considering that every part of me was screaming to stay.

"Did you hear me, Lina? I can go to your house," Aiden repeated.

That was a very bad idea. I had a feeling Aiden wouldn't be so keen on leaving immediately after sex – not because he wanted to cuddle or spend the night with me but because who the hell wanted to leave a warm bed late at night when it was that frackin' cold out – and I didn't have a clue how to ask him to leave without hurting his feelings. And then he'd end up spending the night and I would start to think it meant something and my carefully-constructed plan to not let my pesky feelings get in the way would fall to pieces.

"Now why on earth would I want to stay at my place when you have all this?" I grinned at him. "I have a double bed with the springs starting to poke through and one bathroom with a leaky shower. I'll take the multiple showerheads, thanks."

"You don't stay long enough to even use the shower," he muttered.

I ignored his comment and glanced at the alarm clock. Speaking of which, I had stayed half an hour – fifteen minutes longer then I should have. I needed to leave.

I started to wiggle away from Aiden's delightfully warm body and his arm clamped around my waist in a tight grip. "Don't leave yet."

"I have to," I said before kissing the tip of his nose. "It's getting late."

"It's ten-thirty," he said grumpily. "That's not late."

"I'm not really a night owl," I said before tugging on his arm. "Let me up, Aiden."

He held me more closely and I sighed loudly. "Aiden, I need to – "

"Tomorrow is New Years' Eve," he interrupted. "Why don't you let me take you for dinner and then we can come back to my place and celebrate the new year together."

He nuzzled my neck and I rubbed his forearm. "That sounds like a lot of fun but I already have plans."

He stiffened against me. "Doing what?"

"Tracy and I are going to that new nightclub over on Fifth Avenue."

"That place is nothing but a meat market," he snapped.

"Have you been there?" I asked.

"A few times. The guys who go there are only looking for one thing."

I laughed. "Then it's just like every other nightclub in the city."

I pulled his arm away and slid out of the bed before starting to dress. Aiden was staring at me with something that almost resembled hurt on his face, and I slipped my shirt over my head before sitting on the side of the bed. "What's wrong?"

"Nothing," he said. "I guess I just assumed we would be spending New Years together."

"Why would we?" I asked.

He didn't reply and I stroked his bare chest. "I'm really sorry, Aiden. Honestly, I thought you would be going to Joe's and Stephanie's. You got the email invite to their party, didn't you?"

He nodded. "Yeah, but Susan's still there. I figured it would be best not to go."

"Ooh, good call," I laughed.

"We could go together," he said suddenly. "Susan knows that we're…"

He trailed off and I winked at him. "Fucking like bunnies?"

"What do you say?" He said. "We could still have dinner and then go to Joe's and Steph's after."

"I can't bail on Tracy," I said.

"She could go with us."

I laughed again. "Yeah, Tracy's not really into the whole outdoors scene. She'll be miserable and besides, she's been looking forward to checking out the nightclub."

I stood and Aiden took my hand. "What are your plans for the rest of the weekend?"

"I'm not sure yet," I said. "Probably lying on the couch recovering from my hangover on Saturday and I might check out the animal shelter on Sunday."

I refused to ask him if he wanted to get together. I had already decided I wouldn't contact him on the weekend. Even though the thought of spending the entire weekend in his bed was incredibly tempting I couldn't be too clingy. Aiden wouldn't like that and it would probably make him think I wanted more than what he was willing to give me.

"You're going to be drinking tomorrow night?" He scowled.

"Yes," I said. "Don't worry, I won't drink and drive."

"That's not what I'm worried about," he said.

I gave him a confused look before kissing him lightly. "I really have to go. I'll see you tomorrow at the office."

Chapter 12

"I thought you were going to bail on me, Lina," Tracy shouted into my ear.

"Why?" I shouted over the loud music blaring through the club.

Tracy shrugged. "I figured you'd be spending tonight with Mr. Hot and Horny Boss."

"Why would I? We're not dating."

"How's that going by the way?" Tracy asked. "Still keeping things casual?"

I nodded. "Yes. I don't even spend the night at his place."

"He makes you leave after sex?" Tracy frowned at me

"No, of course not. I leave because I want to. He's just looking for sex so why would I stay after?" I said. "I've only got a few weeks with him anyway so there's no point in getting used to sleeping in his bed. Although – he has a massive tub and a huge walk-in shower with multiple showerheads. I really need to try those out before we're done."

"So now you have a time limit on your fucking?" Tracy shouted just as the music ended.

It was very loud in the beat of silence before the next song began and the two guys sitting at the table next to us glanced over. I blushed and the blond one grinned and winked at me as Tracy poked me in the side.

"Why do you only have a few weeks?" She asked.

"Because Aiden says his flings only last a month," I replied. "So I've got a month to fuck his brains out before he moves on to his next conquest."

"Romantic," Tracy snorted.

"It's not supposed to be," I replied. "Remember?"

"Yeah, although he's a fool if he dumps you after a month. You look fucking hot and the guys in the nightclub have been drooling over you all night."

I laughed. "Thanks, sweetie, but we both know it's you they're drooling over. You're looking sexy as hell, tonight."

"When you've got it, you've got it," Tracy smoothed the front of her bright yellow dress before eyeing me critically. "But seriously, Lina, you look amazing."

"Thanks! You don't think the dress is too tight?"

She shook her head and studied the black dress I was wearing. "Hell, no. It makes your tits look fucking awesome."

I blew her a kiss. "You're so sweet. Although, just between you and me, this bra is killing me. It does wonders in helping the girls defy gravity but I'm pretty sure I'll have permanent bruises from the underwire."

"Beauty hurts, baby," Tracy said. "It's more than just that though. You seem different now."

I shrugged. "I'm still the same old me."

"I know, but you have a dose of, I don't know, confidence I guess. Like you know exactly how hot you are and what to do with it."

"Now that you mention it – I am pretty confident in my hotness," I said with a grin.

She flagged down the server carrying a tray of bright blue shots and took four before handing him some cash. She passed two of them to me and we each held one up.

"To casual fucking," Tracy said. "The best kind of fucking there is."

I laughed and we clinked glasses before I downed the shot. It was surprisingly sweet and I licked my lips before grabbing the second one. Tonight I would get drunk with my best friend, celebrate the beginning of a new year, and not think once about my boss.

* * *

"What's your guy's name again?" I had my mouth pressed against Tracy's ear and I hoped to God the dark-haired Adonis standing next to her didn't hear me.

She whispered something I didn't understand and I gave her a 'what the hell did you just say' look.

"Dwayne!" She shouted into my ear. "As in – dwain the bathtub, I'm dwowning!"

I burst into loud peals of laughter as Tracy grinned at me and accepted the shot of liquor from Dwayne. His blond-haired friend handed me a shot and I smiled at him.

"Thank you, Cody."

"You're welcome, Tina," he said.

"Lina," I said. "It's Lina, not Tina."

"What?" He cupped his hand to his ear.

"LINA! My name is Lina, not Tina!" I screamed.

"Oh, sorry!" He shouted back and I waved my hand at him in a 'don't worry' gesture before raising my glass.

The four of us drank our shots and Tracy, weaving slightly, giggled before setting her empty glass on the table.

"You are so drunk," I said.

"I'm not! I'm only a little drunk," she giggled to Dwayne before wrapping her arm around his thick waist.

He nuzzled her neck and I rolled my eyes when she cupped his face and kissed him firmly on the mouth. They made out enthusiastically and I gave Cody an embarrassed grin. He winked at me before poking Dwayne in the back.

"Hey, get a room, why don't you?"

"Sorry!" Tracy was breathless and her cheeks were flushed from more than just the alcohol.

"What time is it?" She asked suddenly.

I squinted at my cell phone. "Almost eleven."

"An hour to midnight!" Tracy shouted in delight. "Hey, what are you two handsome boys doing after midnight?"

Dwayne stroked the small of her back. "What do you want us to do, baby?"

"Go to Marv's Diner with us," Tracy said promptly. "They have an all night buffet on New Years and I'm starving."

Dwayne grinned at her. "We can do that."

Cody stepped toward me and I took a nervous step back. He was handsome enough with his blond hair and blue eyes but I wasn't the least bit interested in him. Not because I cared for Aiden, I told myself, but because I had promised I wouldn't date anyone else while I was sleeping with him.

Doesn't mean you can't do a little flirting. C'mon, Lina, have a little fun tonight. You can count on one hand the number of men who have been interested in you. Live a little and flirt with the guy!

Part of me wanted to but I found myself taking another step back when Cody leaned toward me and his gaze dropped to my cleavage. I shuffled backward again, wincing when I stepped on someone's foot, and swung around to apologize.

"I'm so sorry, I – "

I blinked at the man standing in front of me. "Aiden? What are you doing here?"

"Celebrating New Years with a few friends," he said.

I glanced around. "Friends? Where?"

He shrugged. "I lost them in the crowd about half an hour ago."

"Oh." I stared dumbly at him. He was wearing a leather jacket, a form fitting white t-shirt and a snug pair of jeans. He looked amazing and smelled fucking delicious. I wanted to rub my fingers against his stubble, I wanted to press a kiss against his mouth. Hell, I wanted to hook my legs around him and climb him like a damn tree.

Aiden was staring at my exposed cleavage and when he lifted his head and stared at me with his hot gaze, I could feel my nipples hardening and my pussy dampening. Fuck, what that man could do to me with one look.

"You look beautiful tonight, Lina," he said.

"Thank you. You look very handsome," I said.

I had forgotten completely about Cody still standing behind me and I jerked when he tapped me on the back.

"Everything okay, Tina?"

I turned to face him and forced myself to smile. "It's Lina and yes, everything's fine," I replied.

He studied Aiden over my shoulder and I jerked again when I felt Aiden's arm slide around my waist. He pulled me tightly against him and dipped his head to press a warm kiss against my mouth.

"Aren't you going to introduce me to your new friend?" He asked with a raised eyebrow.

"Uh, right, of course. Aiden, this is Cody. Cody this is my, uh…"

"Boss," Aiden said smoothly. "Aiden Wright."

He held his hand out and Cody shook it briefly. "Yeah, nice to meetcha."

Aiden held his hand out to Tracy. "You must be Tracy. I'm Aiden Wright. It's nice to meet you."

Tracy looked him up and down before grinning widely. "Oh, it's really nice to meet you, Aiden. Lina didn't tell me you would be here tonight."

"Happy coincidence," Aiden said.

"How fun!" Tracy said brightly. "Why don't you have a few drinks with us?"

"Thanks but I'm driving tonight," Aiden said.

"Bummer for you," Tracy said gravely. "Would you like to hang out with us for a while?"

"Tracy, he's here with friends and he doesn't want to – "

"I'd love to," Aiden interrupted me. "Thanks, Tracy."

"You're welcome," she said with a small grin.

"Aiden, it was really great to see you," I tried to pry myself free of his tight grip and gave up after only a few seconds. "But I'm sure you want to find your friends."

He shook his head and his arm tightened around my waist as he gave Cody a cool look. "No, I'm good right here."

* * *

"How much have you had to drink, Lina?" Aiden's low voice spoke in my ear and I shivered all over as I smiled at the bartender and handed him a few bills. It was close to midnight and when Aiden had excused himself to use the restroom, I had slipped away to the bar. I needed a drink and a moment alone. Aiden showing up at the nightclub had rattled me badly.

"Why are you here, Aiden?" I asked before taking a sip of the whiskey I had ordered.

It was quieter at the bar, the music not quite so loud and jarring, and I forced a smile on my lips as I turned to face my boss.

"I was worried you would do something you'd regret."

"Like what?"

"Like that asshole Cody."

I rolled my eyes. "I wasn't going to *do* anyone tonight. And Cody seemed perfectly nice until you scared him away."

"I didn't scare him away," Aiden said before crowding me against the bar. We were surrounded by people but I forgot about them as I stared into Aiden's dark gaze.

He pressed his mouth against my ear. "I don't want you forgetting that your pussy belongs to me, princess."

"I haven't," I breathed.

"Good. Because it's mine and only mine. You're not going to let that idiot Cody or anyone else in this bar near your tight pussy. Are you?"

I shook my head and he grinned tightly at me.

"Why is that?"

"Because it's yours," I whispered.

"Good girl," he said softly before rubbing my lower back with his hard hand. "How are you getting home tonight?"

"I – what?" I blinked in surprise at the sudden change in topic.

"How are you getting home tonight?" He repeated.

"We're taking a cab."

"No," he shook his head. "I'm going to drive Tracy home and then I'm driving you home. Do you know what will happen next?"

I swallowed thickly and shook my head.

"I'm going to take you into your bedroom, strip off this amazing dress and fuck the pussy that belongs to me."

"Aiden," I whispered. "I don't think – "

"I'm going to fuck you until you're screaming my name and begging me not to stop, kitten," Aiden said. "I've been thinking about fucking you since the moment you left my bed last night."

I blew my breath out in a shaky sigh. I was turned on – fuck, I was soaking wet and ready for Aiden to take me right here in the damn bar – but I was also oddly relieved. Aiden had shown up because he wanted sex, no other reason. I wouldn't have to spend the rest of the night wondering if it was because of something else and that was a good thing. I wasn't feeling a trickle of disappointment, I wasn't.

I took another deep breath and pasted a smile on my face. "That sounds like fun."

"Fun?" He growled. "Fucking me is fun for you?"

"Yes?" I said slowly.

He was giving me an angry look that I didn't understand but before I could question him about it, the crowds of people started to count down from ten. I held Aiden's gaze as his arm slipped around my waist and he pulled me flush against his hard body. I could feel the bulge of his erection and, despite the people around us, I rubbed against him.

His nostrils flared and his hand briefly squeezed my ass before his gaze dropped to my mouth. As the clock struck midnight and people screamed and cheered loudly, Aiden said, "Happy New Year, Lina," before taking my mouth in a hard and punishing kiss.

I returned his kiss eagerly, sliding my tongue into his mouth and pressing my body against his in a shameless display of need. He squeezed my ass again before reaching up and cupping my breast. His thumb worried my nipple into a hard point and he kissed me roughly as I moaned happily into his mouth.

When we finally broke apart, I was breathless with need. Aiden took one look at my flushed face before growling, "We find Tracy and leave. Now, Lina."

I took his hand without argument as he led me through the crowd of people celebrating.

* * *

"This isn't my house." Tracy sat up in the back seat of Aiden's SUV and blinked blearily before yawning.

"Aiden had to make a quick stop," I said. We were parked on the street in front of his building and I craned my head to stare at Tracy.

"Don't puke, Trace,"

"I won't," she said cheerily. "I'm drunk but I'm not that drunk."

She yawned again. "Did you have fun tonight, honey?"

"Yes," I said. "Did you?"

She nodded. "Yeah, Dwayne gave me his number. I might call him. He seemed nice."

"Good, I'm glad."

"He's one hell of a kisser, that's for sure. I should have taken him home."

I laughed. "No you shouldn't have. You need to make those types of decisions when you're sober."

"Party pooper," she pouted at me. "You're going to get laid tonight, I don't see why I shouldn't."

Before I could reply the back door opened and King jumped into the back seat. Tracy shrieked in terror and cringed against the door when King leaned forward and licked her face.

"What the fuck? Why does he have a fucking bear?" She shouted.

I laughed hysterically as King dropped down on to the seat and rested his massive head in Tracy's lap. "He's not a bear."

"Oh my God, his head weighs a ton," Tracy replied. She petted the top of King's head gingerly as Aiden climbed behind the wheel in a blast of cold air and slammed the door shut.

"What's your address, Tracy?" He asked.

She recited it to him and he headed toward her house. He rested his hand on my thigh, his thumb caressing my nylons lightly and just that light touch lit up my nerve endings.

"You know, Aiden," Tracy said conversationally. "I can see why my girl is fucking you. You're damn hot."

"Tracy!" I glared at her as she grinned at me.

"What? He is. I mean, you said he was hot but you really don't understand it until you see him in person."

"You think I'm hot?" Aiden grinned at me and I rolled my eyes.

"You know I do."

"Maybe, but it's still nice to hear."

"Oh please," Tracy said. "You know you're gorgeous. How many women slipped their panties into your pocket tonight?"

"The only panties in my pocket tonight belong to Lina," Aiden said.

"Lina! Why you dirty little tart!" Tracy squealed.

"He's lying, Tracy," I said before giving Aiden a dirty look. "I'm wearing my underwear."

"Sure you are," Tracy said.

"I am!" I insisted. "Tell her the truth, Aiden."

"She is," Aiden said. "But Tuesday was a different story."

"Aiden!" I hissed.

"Ooh, what happened on Tuesday?"

Aiden grinned at Tracy in the rear view mirror. "I definitely had Lina's panties in my pocket on Tuesday."

"You're boinking at the office? Lina, you didn't tell me you were boinking at the office," Tracy said. "Fuck, that's hot."

"We're not boinking at the office," I said. "We didn't actually have sex on Tuesday, we just..."

I trailed off, my cheeks flaming bright red as Aiden laughed and Tracy squealed again. "I want details."

"No," I said firmly.

"Well you're no fun at all," Tracy said. "Here I was thinking you were having sex at the office."

"Technically we have," Aiden said cheerfully.

"Aiden, shut up!" I said.

He shrugged, "What? We have. The night of the Christmas party – or did you forget?"

"If she forgot that doesn't look good for you, my friend," Tracy said brightly. "You might want to work harder."

"I didn't forget," I said. "I just prefer not to talk about my sexual activities with a group of people.

"Group of people? Please, I'm your best friend," Tracy said. "Besides, I already know most of the details."

She reached out and patted Aiden's shoulder. "Good on you, honey, for not insisting that Lina has to come from your dick stick. It's so annoying when men think their penises are magic climax inducers."

Aiden burst out laughing and Tracy snickered as I slapped my hand over my eyes.

"Oh my God," I moaned. "Pull the car over, Aiden."

"Why?"

"Because I'm going to kill Tracy and I don't want to get blood splatter on your leather seats."

"What are you killing me for?" Tracy said indignantly. "You're the one who said Aiden was the best lover you've ever had. Although," she patted Aiden's shoulder again, "not to rain on your parade or anything but it probably wouldn't have taken much to be better than that jackass Kent. That man couldn't find a woman's clit if you gave him a flashlight and a map."

Aiden laughed again and Tracy grinned delightedly at him. "I also hear that you have a magic tongue."

"Tracy, if you don't shut up, I really will murder you," I said through gritted teeth.

"Honestly, I'm enjoying hearing about how amazing you think I am in bed," Aiden said.

"She used a lot of very flattering adjectives to describe your bedroom abilities," Tracy said solemnly.

"Like what?" Aiden asked.

"Tracy," I warned.

"Let's see," Tracy said, "I believe awesome was used, fantastic, unbelievable, incredible, oh and earth-shattering was tossed around as well."

"Nice," Aiden said before squeezing my thigh. "I think you're earth-shattering in bed too, Lina."

"Thanks," I muttered as Tracy sighed happily.

"That's so sweet. I told Lina repeatedly that she wasn't the problem in bed, it was that butthead Kent, but she never believed me. I'm glad you made her realize that Kent was the issue."

She sighed again and leaned back in the seat before stroking King's head lightly. "You two are just so cute together."

"Tracy?" I said.

"Yeah?"

"Can you please stop talking now?"

"Sure," she said agreeably.

Ten minutes later we were parked in front of her apartment building and I unclicked my seatbelt. "I'm just going to walk her to her apartment, I'll be right back."

"I don't need you to walk me to my apartment," Tracy said. "I'm not that drunk."

"Tracy, I'm not comfortable with – "

"I'll text you as soon as I'm in the apartment," she said. She unbuckled her seat belt, shoved King's head off her lap and leaned over the front seat to kiss me on the cheek.

"I love you, honey."

"I love you too," I said.

She tapped her cheek and grinned at Aiden. "Plant one on me, handsome."

He pressed a polite kiss to her cheek and she winked at him. "Be sweet to my girl tonight, okay?"

"I will."

She slid out of the car and I rolled my window down. "I'm not leaving until I get your text so make sure you text me as soon as you're in the apartment."

"Will do," she said breezily before, weaving slightly, walking into her apartment building.

I pulled my cell phone out of my purse and gave Aiden an embarrassed smile. "I'm sorry."

"For what?"

"For giving Tracy details of, uh, what we did in bed. I shouldn't have done that."

He shrugged. "It doesn't bother me."

"Are you sure?"

"Yes," he replied. "Do you really think I have a magic tongue?"

I blushed and stared at my phone. "There's definitely witchcraft involved."

He laughed and squeezed my thigh again as my cell buzzed.

"She's in her apartment," I said. "We can go."

Leaving his hand on my thigh, he pulled into the street as King hung his head over the seat and licked my face. I wiped the drool from my cheek before scratching his wide head. "Why did you stop and pick up King?"

"I was out for most of the day," he said casually. "Figured he was tired of being alone at home."

"Oh, right. That makes sense," I replied before staring out the window. For a moment I had thought he was planning on staying the night with me and a weird combination of panic and happiness had swept through me. I didn't have the guts to ask him to leave after sex – it just seemed so...rude, I guess – but I was worrying for nothing anyway. Aiden wouldn't want to stay any longer than he had to in my tiny house.

I actually really liked my house, but it needed lots of repairs that were beyond my capability and my budget and if you compared it to Aiden's penthouse, it was definitely a bit of a dump. I sighed again and stared blankly out the window as Aiden drove.

* * *

"This is nice," Aiden said.

I laughed and slipped out of my heels as he studied my small bedroom.

"Did you know you're missing baseboard along that wall?" He asked politely.

I nodded. "Yeah, it just fell off one day. I tried to nail it back on, but I split the baseboard in half. I went to the hardware store to buy more but the house is on the older side and the baseboards are a weird size that they don't make anymore. I'm going to have to replace all of the baseboards in the room but," I pointed to the other side of the room where half of the baseboard was torn off, "when I started to take off that baseboard, it ripped a hole in the drywall."

He stared at me and I blushed before shrugging. "I'm not really handy like you are. Plus, I want to paint the bedroom anyway so I figured I'll paint it first then when I have a little extra money, I'll hire someone to fix the drywall and put in the new baseboards."

He took off his jacket and draped it over the chair in the corner as King wandered to Rex's bed. I hadn't thrown it away, it hurt too much, and he sniffed at it gingerly before woofing softly and lying down on it. He rubbed his face against the fabric, his tail wagging madly, and I swallowed down the pang of loss. I really needed to get another dog. It would help with the loneliness when my month with Aiden was finished.

"Lina?" Aiden had stripped off his shirt and he touched my upper back lightly. "Is there something wrong?"

"No," I said. "Well, other than the fact that my bed is not nearly as comfortable as yours."

He laughed and slid down the zipper on the back of my dress. "I don't care."

"You say that now," I said, "but wait until…"

My voice died out in a whispery moan as Aiden dipped his head and licked down my spine. I moaned and staggered back a little.

"How drunk are you, Lina?" Aiden asked suddenly.

"Not that drunk. Why?"

"I'm not in the habit of taking advantage of women who've had too much to drink," he said.

I laughed. "I have a nice buzz going, nothing more. You're not taking advantage of me. You know I want you."

"I want you too," he whispered before kissing the back of my neck.

I leaned against him. I was feeling very warm and relaxed thanks to the alcohol and Aiden's touch, and I helped him ease my dress down before stepping out of it.

"You look so beautiful tonight, Lina," Aiden whispered.

"Thank you," I said. I couldn't stop my moan of relief when Aiden unhooked my bra. I took my first deep breath of the night, moaning again, and Aiden touched the deep marks the material had left in my skin.

"Jesus, Lina," he said. "This looks incredibly painful."

I shrugged. "Gravity is not my friend."

I inhaled sharply when Aiden's tongue traced the grooves in my skin. He kissed and nuzzled the skin lightly.

"I think this is starting to bruise," he said.

"Probably. I'm a bruiser, remember?" I giggled a little. "Bruiser…"

He kissed me and I sighed happily at the feel of his warm tongue. His hand slipped into my panties and he rubbed my clit firmly.

"So wet, Lina," he said in a low rasp.

"You do that to me," I said.

"Good," he growled before kissing me again.

"Aiden," I moaned when he finally stopped, "Don't tease me tonight, please? I need you."

"I need you too, Lina," he whispered. "So much."

We undressed each other quickly and I straddled Aiden's hips when he stretched out on the bed.

"I want to be on top, okay?"

He nodded and rubbed my wide hips with his warm hands. "Whatever you want, kitten."

He helped me guide his cock into my pussy and we both groaned as I sank slowly down his thick length. When he was fully inside of me, I cupped my breasts and rubbed lightly at my nipples. Aiden made a harsh groan of need and I smiled at the look of hunger in his eyes.

"Do you want me, Aiden?"

"You know I do,"

"I want you too," I said. I rocked on his cock, moving slowly and deliberately as he stared up at me. I braced my hands on his chest and kept up the same slow pace as Aiden's hips rose to meet my gentle thrusts. I had never been this relaxed in bed before. I decided it was probably a combination of the alcohol and my growing belief that Aiden found me sexy in bed no matter what, and I leaned down and brushed my breasts against his hard chest before kissing him.

"It feels so good, Aiden," I whispered.

"Yes," he agreed. "You're so tight, kitten."

I reached for his hands, pinning them above his head and linking our fingers together as I continued to brush my nipples against him. I moved my pelvis in a slow up and down motion and then bit my lip at the sudden burst of pleasure.

"Lina?" Aiden frowned as I slowed to a stop and stared wide-eyed at him. "What's wrong? Did I hurt you?"

I shook my head. "No, it doesn't hurt, Aiden. It feels different and – and good."

I repeated the motion, my pussy clamping around his dick when an even stronger bolt of pleasure flooded my pelvis.

"OH!" I said. "Oh, God. What was that?"

"You're going to make me come if you keep squeezing like that, Lina," Aiden said in a strangled voice. "Ease up, princess."

"No," I said. "I want more."

I closed my eyes and rode him slowly, squeaking with delight at each pulse of pleasure that spread through my body. I could feel his cock brushing against the front wall of my pussy and I rubbed harder against him.

"Oh," I moaned, "Oh, oh, oh."

"Lina!" Aiden muttered. "Lina, please, I can't hold off much longer."

I ignored him and rode him faster and harder. I was panting and moaning and squealing shamelessly, and I shrieked when the exquisite pleasure radiated through my entire body. Aiden groaned, his hands clamping down on mine with painful intensity as his body shuddered beneath me and his hips bucked wildly.

I rode him through his release, my eyes squeezed shut and my body shaking with pleasure until he collapsed under me. I eased off of him, my legs were like jelly, and fell on to the bed.

"Lina? Are you okay?" He leaned over me and stroked my stomach gently.

I forced my eyes open and gave him a thoroughly satisfied grin. "I am fucking fantastic, Aiden."

He laughed and placed a light kiss on my nipple before resting his head on my upper chest. "Good."

"I just had an orgasm from sex," I announced.

"Yes, I know. I was there."

I smiled dreamily and held up my hand. "High-five."

He laughed again and slapped his hand against mine before rolling me to my side. He pulled up the sheet and the quilt and tucked them firmly around our bodies.

"I have no idea how that happened but I want to do it again and again," I said.

"I'm going to need at least ten minutes, princess."

I made a soft noise of happiness. "Tired. Tomorrow, okay?"

"Okay." He nuzzled the back of my neck.

I was almost asleep when I finally comprehended that Aiden was still in the bed with me. "Aiden?"

"Yes?"

"Are you leaving?"

"Do you want me to?"

I shook my head. I was so tired and Aiden's body was delightfully warm against mine. "No, but I'll understand if you want to go."

"I want to stay," he whispered into my hair. "Good night, Lina."

"Night, Aiden."

Chapter 13

When I woke the next morning, Aiden's side of the bed was cold and I bit back my sigh of disappointment. It was for the best. I shouldn't have let him stay the night in the first place, I reminded myself.

I grabbed my robe and wrapped it around me before heading to the bathroom. It was just after ten and my mouth tasted like a dead possum, but at least I didn't have a headache and my stomach felt fine. I would have a hot shower – I said a silent prayer that the damn thing would actually work this morning – eat something and call Tracy to check on her.

I swung open the door of the bathroom and made a shrill cry of surprise when Aiden grinned at me from the tub.

"Morning, princess. How are you feeling?"

"Wh- what are you doing?"

He was standing in my tub and I stared at the wrench in his hands as he tightened something above the shower head.

"Fixing your shower," he said.

"What? Where did you get that?" I motioned to the wrench in his hand.

"You have a toolbox in the basement," he replied. "You didn't know that?"

"It must have been Kent's," I said and then hurried on when a dark look crossed his face. "Is that the new showerhead?"

"Yes. I threw the other one away – you were right, it was trashed – and hooked up your new one."

"Aiden," I said weakly. "You – you shouldn't have done that."

"I don't mind," he said. "I like fixing things, remember?"

"Well, yes, but – "

I squealed when King's wet nose rubbed against the back of my knees. "King, stop that!"

He woofed and licked my calf before padding down the hall and disappearing into the kitchen. Aiden stepped out of the tub and turned on the taps. I watched in amazement as a steady stream of water came out of the showerhead.

"Holy shit," I said. "That's amazing."

He laughed and picked up the other tools strewn about on the vanity. "You're welcome. Now, why don't you have a shower and I'll make us some breakfast."

"You don't have to make breakfast," I said. "I usually just have toast and coffee and – "

"I don't mind," he repeated before leaning down to kiss me.

I jerked my head back and he scowled at me.

"You don't want to kiss me before I brush my teeth. Trust me," I said.

He laughed and pressed a quick kiss against my mouth. "Hurry up in the shower, Lina. We have some errands to run."

"What? What errands?"

"You'll see," he said. He shut the bathroom door and I stared blankly at the closed door before reaching for my toothbrush.

* * *

"Aiden," I protested, "you really don't have to do this."

"I know," he said as he carefully fit a new piece of drywall into the hole on the wall.

It was two hours later. After breakfast we had driven to the Home Depot and I had watched in disbelief as Aiden picked up supplies for both the drywall and the baseboards. He had insisted I pick out a paint colour for my bedroom and had refused to allow me to pay for any of it.

"Seriously," I said. "You must have better things to do on your Saturday."

"Like what?" He asked.

"Sex," I said.

He laughed and winked at me. "Later, princess. Have you finished taping?"

I nodded and he slapped me lightly on the ass. "Then start painting. You won't be able to paint this wall until after I sand it tomorrow afternoon but you can get the rest of it finished."

"I'd rather be having sex," I said grumpily.

"If you're a good girl and paint, I'll eat your pussy later," he said.

Shamefully enough, that got me picking up the paint roller and moving to the far side of the room. "You have to at least let me pay you for the supplies."

"Why? I'm rich, remember?"

"That doesn't mean you need to be paying for my home improvements."

"You can pay me in blowjobs," he said teasingly.

I grinned at him as I painted the far wall. "See, now that sounds like a good deal but if I give you a blowjob for every home improvement you do, I'll end up with, I dunno, lockjaw or something. I love my little house but it's kind of falling apart."

"Next weekend I'll fix your back door and the leaky kitchen faucet," he promised.

"That's really sweet but I'm not around next weekend," I said.

"Where are you going?" He said quickly.

"I'm visiting my sister Kate. I took Friday off, remember?"

He shook his head. "I didn't remember. How long are you gone?"

"I leave Thursday night after work and come back Sunday night. Don't worry, I'm only missing one day of work." I grinned at him but he didn't return my smile.

"You're gone the entire weekend?"

"Yes. What's wrong?"

He had that stubborn, almost pouting, look on his face again.

"Nothing," he said. "What are you and your sister going to do?"

"Well, I know we're having dinner at her best friend's house on Sunday but other than that we don't have solid plans. Kate's single too so we'll probably go out to the bar at least once. She's absolutely gorgeous – she got lucky and inherited my mother's red hair and her metabolism – and the men flock to her like a herd of turtles."

I stared critically at the wall I was painting. "God, I suck at painting. I probably should have taped more of the ceiling, I can't cut-in to save my life."

I squeaked in surprise when Aiden's hard body pressed against me and his hand slipped into my pants. He cupped my pussy possessively and nipped my neck. "You're going out to the bar?"

"Probably," I moaned as his rough fingers rubbed at my clit.

"Are you going to be a good girl and remember that you belong to me?" He asked.

I hesitated and he growled before sliding his middle finger into my already-wet pussy."

"Lina," he said, "when those assholes at the bar hit on you – "

"They won't hit on me," I interrupted as I squirmed on his hand, "not with Kate around."

He nipped me again on the neck. "When they hit on you are you going to remember that your pussy belongs to me?"

This time I nodded. His statement that I belonged to him had sent a funny little thrill up my spine. He often said my pussy belonged to him, - hell, it was practically his mantra at this point – but this was different. It seemed more intimate, more like we were in a relationship, and I berated myself internally as Aiden rubbed his erection against my ass.

It doesn't mean anything, Lina. Aiden's just doing his usual alpha male thing. The guy likes to mark his territory and that's you. That's all you'll ever be to him and don't forget it.

Aiden kissed the side of my neck and slid his hand out of my pants. "Good."

"Aiden?" I squeezed his arm when he tried to step away. "You are seriously not stopping now."

"Of course I am," he said cheekily. "You've got painting to do, remember?"

"Don't take this the wrong way but you're a tease, Aiden Wright," I said.

He laughed and pinched me on the ass before pointing to the wall. "Paint now, pussy eating later."

* * *

I sat down on the couch and stared blankly at the TV. As promised, Aiden had taken me to bed after we finished painting. He had spent nearly an hour with his face buried between my thighs. I was weak and trembling from multiple orgasms and begging him to fuck me by the time he was finished. He had taken me roughly and I had been a little disappointed that I didn't have an orgasm from sex alone. I had wanted to, had even tried riding Aiden like I had the night before, but just as I was starting to feel frustrated and inadequate, he had reached between us and rubbed my clit until I had climaxed. I was just falling asleep when Aiden had kissed me gently, dressed and left.

I sighed and flipped aimlessly through the channels. I wasn't feeling depressed and lonely, I told myself. I hadn't even expected to see Aiden this weekend so spending last night and most of today with him had been a bonus.

I glanced at my watch before standing. It was close to dinner and I decided I would have a bite to eat and watch a movie on Netflix. My cell phone buzzed and I pulled it out of my pocket, my heart speeding up when I saw the text from Aiden.

Chinese or pizza for dinner?
What?
Do you want Chinese or pizza for dinner?
You're picking up dinner?
Yes.
For us?
Yes, Ms. Jones.

I could almost hear the annoyance in his text and a small smile crossed my face as I texted back.

It doesn't matter to me.

Good. Open the door.

A frown on my face, I scurried down the hall and opened the door. King bounded past me, pausing to lick my hand, before disappearing into the kitchen. Aiden was standing on the front porch, a six pack of beer in one hand and a large pizza box in the other.

"You already picked up dinner?"

He grinned. "I did."

"What if I had wanted Chinese food?" I asked as he shouldered past me and headed to the kitchen.

"Do you?" He asked.

I followed him into the kitchen. "No, pizza is good. Aiden, what are you doing here?"

"Having dinner with you?" He arched his eyebrow at me as he pulled plates from the cupboard.

"But you left earlier and I thought..."

I trailed off and he gave me a quizzical look. "Thought what, Ms. Jones?"

"Well, that we were done for the weekend," I said lamely.

He shrugged. "I wanted to pick up a change of clothes and some food for King."

For the first time I noticed the overnight bag on his shoulder. He dropped it to the table before pulling out a large Ziplock baggie filled with dog food. He studied Rex's empty food dish in the corner.

"Would it be okay if I used Rex's food dish to feed King? I forgot to bring his dishes."

I nodded and he poured a healthy amount of food into the dish. King, drooling profusely, buried his face into the bowl and ate enthusiastically as Aiden filled Rex's water dish and set it next to the food dish.

"Sorry, he's bad for drooling," he said as he mopped up the trail of saliva with paper towel.

"It's fine," I said. "Aiden, you didn't have to come back. I know you have a busy life and – "

"God, I'm starving," he said, ignoring me completely. "Do you want two slices or three?"

"Uh, two is fine," I replied. "Aiden, are you sure you want to hang out with me tonight?"

"Did you have other plans?" He suddenly asked. "Going back out to the bar with Tracy perhaps?"

"Of course not," I said. "Tracy's still recovering from her hangover. I was just going to have a bite to eat and watch a movie on Netflix."

"Sounds like fun," he said cheerfully. He handed me my plate of pizza. "I hope you like pepperoni and mushroom."

"I do." I followed him into the living room and he set his plate of pizza and the beer on the coffee table before handing me the remote.

"Pick a movie, princess."

* * *

"That movie was terrible," Aiden announced as I shut off the TV. "You're never allowed to pick the movie again."

"It wasn't that bad," I said.

"Are you kidding? If I had known you were going to pick some third-rate, low-budget horror movie with truly appalling special effects, I would have picked the movie."

"Whatever," I laughed. "If you think I didn't hear you scream like a girl when the serial killer popped up out of the bushes, you're wrong."

"I didn't scream, Ms. Jones, I merely gasped in surprise at the obviously rubber axe he was wielding."

I laughed again. "What can I say? I have a weakness for bad horror movies."

I grabbed the empty pizza box and carried it into the kitchen. Aiden followed me and I checked the time before smiling at him.

"It's getting pretty late so I guess I'll talk to you later?"

He pulled me into his embrace and nuzzled my neck. "Are you asking me to leave, Lina?"

"Uh, well..."

"Here's the thing, Ms. Jones. We have two choices." He cupped my breast and kneaded it gently. "You can send me out into the dark and freezing cold weather and make me drive home on icy and dangerous roads, or we can go to your warm bedroom, get naked, and see if we can make you come from being fucked."

I shivered all over as he pressed kisses against the tender skin of my throat. "Well, which is it, kitten? Option A or option B?"

"B," I said. "Definitely option B."

"Good," he squeezed my ass but before he could lead me from the kitchen I touched his arm.

"Only, I don't think I can do that again, Aiden. At least not without a lot more beer. I tried earlier today and it didn't work. I'm sorry."

He scowled at me. "You don't have to be sorry, Lina."

He cupped my face and forced me to look at him. "Let's make something perfectly clear, princess. I'm not Kent. I'll never expect you to orgasm from sex alone, and you're not to feel frustrated or worried about it if you don't. The only reason I suggested we try again is because it made you feel good and I like making you feel good. Do you understand?"

"Yes," I said.

He lifted my hand to his mouth, brushing his lips across my knuckles before leading me to the bedroom. My legs were shaking and, despite Aiden's assurances, I was already feeling nervous. What if I couldn't do it? What if we tried and kept trying and I just –

"Lina, you're overthinking again," Aiden said quietly.

I took a deep breath. "I know."

He kissed me deeply, his mouth slanting over mine to take what was his, and I wrapped my arms around his waist and clung tightly to him. God, I loved his kisses. I would miss them when this was over. Hell, I would miss everything he did to me and I was terribly afraid that after Aiden, no other man would ever do it for me again.

Stop it, Lina. Thinking that way isn't going to help you relax.

Good point. I concentrated on kissing Aiden, on memorizing every touch of his mouth and his hands, as he peeled off my shirt and then my bra. He cupped my full breasts, teasing the nipples into an aching hardness, before stepping away.

"Hey," I pouted at him, "where are you going?"

"I brought something tonight to help you relax," he said.

"More alcohol?" I wiggled my eyebrows at him and he laughed before rummaging through his bag.

"No, get undressed and lie on your stomach on the bed, Lina,"

I quickly tossed my pants and underwear before lying on my stomach. I pulled the sheet up to cover my ass and twisted my head to stare at Aiden. He was undressing and I admired his flat abdomen and the thick length of his cock as he dropped his pants.

All mine, I thought greedily as a little tingle went through my pussy.

Yes, for now. Don't forget he'll get tired of you soon and –

Shut up! Just shut up!

I forced the voice of reason out of my head and squeezed my eyes shut as Aiden approached the bed. He made a small displeased sound under his breath and I tried not to flinch when he pulled down the sheet and my ass was exposed.

"Your ass is one of my favourite parts of your body, Lina," he said, "you're not to hide it from me."

"I wasn't hiding it, I was just – "

I squealed when he slapped it hard and scowled at him. "That's not relaxing, Aiden."

He laughed. "No, I suppose it isn't, princess. But I do enjoy seeing my handprints on your lovely ass."

He straddled my thighs, pinning me to the bed, and leaned over me to breathe hotly into my ear. "And you like it too, don't you, princess?"

"Yes," I whispered.

His cock was rubbing between my ass cheeks and I stifled my moan of need as he said, "Your ass, like your pussy, belongs to me. Say it, Lina."

"My ass belongs to you," I said as he brushed my dark hair aside and pressed a light kiss against my neck.

"Good girl," he whispered. "My ass to touch," his hands reached down and roamed lightly across my butt, "my ass to spank," his hard slap made me squeal with pleasure, "my ass to fuck."

I tensed, his cock was hard and heavy and still pressed between my ass cheeks and for one moment I was afraid he was about to fuck my ass right now.

"Not tonight, Lina," he whispered, dispelling my fear. "There are a few things that need to be done first."

"Like what?" I asked. I was genuinely curious and I craned my head again to stare at Aiden.

He squeezed my full ass cheeks. "Stretching, mostly. You'll be tight and I don't want to hurt you."

I licked my lips nervously. "Stretching doesn't sound... fun."

He laughed. "I'll make it fun. Trust me, Lina."

I gave him a doubtful look and he bent and pressed a kiss between my shoulder blades. "We'll start with my fingers, then use plugs until I'm sure you can take my cock."

"How long does that take?" I asked.

"It depends. Sometimes a few weeks but it'll be worth it, Lina. Believe me."

"Worth it for you, maybe," I said. "What happens if I don't like it?"

"Then we won't do it," he said. "We'll go slowly, Lina, I promise. I won't fuck your ass until I'm sure you're ready. If that takes weeks or months, so be it. I can wait."

He frowned at the look on my face. "What?"

"Nothing," I said quickly.

I wouldn't be with Aiden in weeks or months so unless my butt had some kind of fast super stretching ability, I didn't have to worry about it. And the trickle of disappointment I was feeling was easy enough to ignore. In fact, it probably wasn't disappointment but relief. Wasn't it? The issue was that I wasn't entirely certain I wanted to have anal sex but I knew I would try it for Aiden. When we were in bed, he had this way of making me forget everything but wanting to please him. It was both thrilling and disturbing to realize that I would do exactly what Aiden wanted.

It doesn't matter, remember? Aiden will be finished with you before you even get to that point.

The smell of vanilla drifted to me and I moaned happily when Aiden's strong hands kneaded my shoulders. They were warm and slippery from the vanilla-scented oil and I made another groan of appreciation.

"A massage?" I murmured.

"Close your eyes and relax, princess," he said.

I did what he asked as he kneaded and rubbed the muscles in my back. He was very thorough and twenty minutes later I was as pliable as a wet noodle and close to dozing.

"Lina," he whispered in my ear.

"Hmm?" I said sleepily.

"Turn over."

I did what he asked, keeping my eyes closed, and I could almost hear the smile in his voice when he said, "My kitten is sleepy now."

"Mm, hmm," I agreed as his warm hands stroked my upper chest. "That feels so good, Aiden."

His hands closed over my breasts and I moaned when he pulled lightly on my nipples. They hardened immediately and he made a low sound of approval as my sleepiness disappeared in a hurry. I opened my eyes and gasped as he pinched each of my nipples before rolling them between his fingertips.

He grinned at me and toyed and teased my nipples until they were coated in oil and I was arching my back for more. His cock rubbed against my stomach and I whimpered with pleasure when he leaned down and sucked on one throbbing nipple.

"Oh," I moaned when he licked the tip and then pulled on it with his teeth. My hands were gripping his hips now, clenching into his firm flesh as he kissed his way up my chest before pressing his mouth against mine.

He tasted like vanilla and I licked eagerly at his lips, loving the sweetness.

"It tastes good," I whispered when he released my mouth.

"Edible massage oil is a rather brilliant invention," he teased against my mouth. "Do you want more?"

"Yes," I said. I tried to kiss him again but he straightened and picked up the bottle before pouring some in the palm of his hand. He slicked it over his cock until it was shiny with oil.

"Sit up, princess."

I struggled into a sitting position, Aiden was still straddling my thighs, and he placed one hand on the back of my neck, kneading it lightly, as he smiled at me. "Open up, kitten."

I opened my mouth eagerly and he guided his cock past my lips. "Be a good girl and lick me clean."

My hands still digging into his hips, I licked and sucked at his cock. The taste of him mixed with the vanilla was intoxicating and I didn't object when Aiden pressed his cock further into my mouth. I took a deep breath and tried to control my gag reflex as he pushed harder. He fucked my mouth in a gentle rhythm, holding me steady with his hand at the back of my neck, and I sucked with enthusiasm despite my watery eyes and the occasional lack of oxygen.

With a harsh groan, he pulled his cock out of my mouth and I leaned forward, trying to take it back.

"No, princess," he said. "I want to be inside you when I come."

My pussy throbbed as he pushed me on to my back and stretched out beside me. His fingers slipped between my legs and a hot flush rose in my cheeks when I realized just how wet I was. My inner thighs were drenched in moisture and my pussy slippery.

He pushed two fingers into my pussy and the liquid dripping from it made it easy for him to thrust steadily in and out despite how hard I tried to grip him with my muscles. His thumb brushed across my clit and I moaned with delight.

He changed the angle of his fingers and I blinked at him when he made a "come here" motion inside of me. It felt strange and sent a weird pressure through my aching core.

"Aiden," I said as he did it again. "What are you – oh!"

My back arched and I grabbed at his wrist as a familiar lightning bolt of pleasure rocketed through my pelvis.

"There it is," he said with a satisfied grin.

"There's what?" I asked.

He didn't reply, just stroked me again and I clamped my mouth shut around the scream that wanted to escape.

"Oh, fuck," I moaned. My fingers dug into his wrist as he rubbed firmly and I writhed against him.

"Aiden, wh-what are you doing to me?" I gasped.

He teased my nipple with his tongue before smiling. "It's your g-spot, princess."

"I – that's a myth," I said breathlessly.

"Is it?" He raised one eyebrow before pressing against the front wall of my pussy with the pads of his fingers. I cried out, my entire body shaking madly under his and tried to wiggle away from him at the intensity of the sensation.

He threw one heavy leg over mine, pinning my legs against the bed as I begged incoherently. I couldn't think, couldn't focus on anything except the sensations coursing through my entire body.

My body was tensing, my nipples were as hard as glass and my hips were thrusting uncontrollably against Aiden's fingers. The pressure was increasing, the ache and the need for release coiling in my belly like a tight ball, and I was so damn close that I knew it would take only one more stroke of Aiden's fingers - just one more touch against that ticking time-bomb of a spot.

Before I could tumble over the edge into the relief I needed, Aiden pulled his fingers away. Hot tears immediately flowed down my cheeks and I pulled on his wrist with a desperation I should have been ashamed of, but wasn't.

"No, oh no, please," I begged, "Why are you stopping?"

"Patience, kitten," he said.

I slapped at his chest, my frustration and my desire overriding my common sense, and hissed at him like an angry cat. "Asshole! Don't you dare fucking stop!"

I clawed his chest with my nails and he flinched before taking my wrists and pinning them above my head as he pushed his body between my thighs.

"Bastard!" I shouted. "I swear to God, I'm going to knee you in the balls for this! I mean it, Aiden! You can't leave me like this, you can't – "

My angry tirade came to a screeching halt when Aiden thrust his cock into my wet pussy. Just having him in me, just having something for my needy and desperate pussy to tighten around, eased some of the ache.

"Better, princess?"

"Not enough," I hissed again at him.

He was still holding my wrists captive above my head and I struggled fiercely when he took both wrists in one hand. Even then, he was too strong for me to escape and I glared angrily at him as he put his free hand on my ass and squeezed it roughly.

"Listen to me, princess," he said. "I'm going to release your wrists. If you try and scratch me again with your little claws, I'll stop fucking you and give you a spanking. Do you understand?"

I scowled and refused to answer. The ache in my pelvis was at a fevered pitch now and I could have cheerfully clawed Aiden's chest to ribbons for denying me my pleasure.

"Answer me," he said before delivering a hard slap to my ass. I squealed and clenched around him, feeling a small thread of satisfaction when Aiden groaned and made two hard and uncontrollable thrusts into me.

"Ohhh," I moaned happily and a small grin crossed his face before he gave me another stern look.

"Are you going to behave, Lina? Is my little kitten going to keep her claws to herself?"

"Yes," I snapped.

"Good girl," he said and I both loved and hated my flush of happiness at pleasing him.

He released my wrists and I clutched at his biceps, trying not to dig my nails into his arms.

"Please, Aiden," I said sweetly. "Please put your fingers in me again."

"You don't like my cock?" He asked before sliding back and forth in an easy rhythm.

"You know I do," I moaned. "But before – it was – oh, please, Aiden."

"God, what you fucking do to me, Lina," he suddenly whispered before straightening to his knees. He took my legs and I muttered a harsh cry of surprise when he lifted them and draped them over his shoulders. I could feel the strain in my thigh muscles and my insecurities were starting to crowd into my head. I wasn't flexible or coordinated enough for this and already my thighs were starting to hurt. Before I could slide my legs down, Aiden was gripping my ass and lifting, supporting most of my lower body weight. The strain on my thighs eased and my legs slid further over his shoulders.

"Okay?" He asked and I nodded but gave him an anxious look.

The guy was going to hurt himself holding me up like that, and I could only imagine what I looked like in this position with my belly pushed out and my large thighs resting against his chest.

"Am I – am I hurting you?" I gasped out as he repositioned me slightly.

"No," he said firmly. "Hang on tight, princess."

"Hang on to what?" I said. "Aiden, what are you going to – "

The thought was lost when Aiden thrust into me and the head of his cock rubbed firmly against my previously believed mythical g-spot. I screamed, my hands clutching at the sheets, as my entire body shuddered against him.

"Hmm, hit it on the first try. Not bad," Aiden said as I gaped at him.

He winked at me. "Did you like that, kitten?"

"Do it again," I begged. "Again, Aiden. Again."

"My pleasure, princess," he said.

My back arched, my toes curling as he thrust back and forth and wave after wave of indescribable pleasure coursed through me. I moaned and screamed and pleaded, my hands yanking at the bed sheets as Aiden continued his relentless pace. My head was thrashing back and forth and I screamed his name as the pleasure crested inside of me and burst. My eyes rolled back in my head and I was only dimly aware of Aiden's warm seed filling my pussy. Aiden released my ass and I collapsed against the bed. He caught my legs as they slid from his shoulders and placed them gently on the bed before lying next to me. I was panting and shuddering uncontrollably and he stroked my stomach and my thighs and pressed kisses against my damp forehead.

After a while, a long while, I opened my eyes and stared up at him. He kissed me, I could still taste vanilla on his mouth, and rested his forehead against mine.

"Holy shit, Aiden," I whispered weakly. "Holy shit."

"My thoughts exactly," he replied before pulling me into his embrace. I rested my head against his chest, listening as the beat of his heart slowed to a steady rhythm, and closed my eyes again.

"Aiden?"

"Yes?"

"I'm sorry for calling you an asshole and a bastard and threatening to knee you in the balls."

He laughed and hugged me tightly. "I know. Go to sleep, Lina."

Chapter 14

"You're sure you're ready for this?" Aiden asked as we parked in the parking lot of the animal shelter.

"I am," I said. "Besides, I'm just going to look today. It's not really practical to adopt a dog before I return from Kate's."

King stuck his head over the seat and licked my hair before slobbering across my cheek.

"King," I scolded him and pushed him back a little. "Stop drooling on me."

He woofed and laid his massive body across the back seat as we climbed out of the SUV.

"Is it too cold for him?" I asked as we crossed the parking lot.

"No," Aiden said. "He'll be fine."

He opened the door and I took a deep breath before stepping into the shelter. The door to the dog kennels was to the left and I stared at it as Aiden took my hand and squeezed it lightly.

"Ready?" He asked again.

I nodded and even though I knew I should be dropping his hand I couldn't bring myself to do it. Holding hands, we walked into the kennel.

* * *

I stared at the dog sitting quietly at the back of the kennel. We had spent the last fifteen minutes slowly walking through the maze of kennels and Aiden had wandered ahead. He was petting a very loud and very enthusiastic poodle through the bars of a kennel and I smiled briefly before staring again at the dog.

She was light gray with a big, blocky head and a white muzzle. I glanced at her information sheet before crouching and making a kissing noise. "Daisy, come here, girl. Come here, Daisy."

She cocked her head at me and I made another kissy noise, secretly delighted when her tail wagged a little and she stood from the blanket she was sitting on. She stretched before walking stiffly toward me. She rested her nose against the bars that separated us and I stuck my fingers between the bars and scratched the side of her head.

She sighed and leaned against my fingers, trapping them between the bars and her head. I winced and tried to pull my fingers free as a voice said above me, "Do you like her? She's a very sweet girl."

I smiled at the woman wearing the bright green shirt of the volunteers as she crouched next to me.

"She seems lovely."

"Oh, she is. She's such a sweetheart. Very gentle and kind," the woman said quickly. "She would make a great companion."

"Why is she in here?" I asked.

"Her family was moving out of state and they didn't want to take her."

"Because she's old?" I asked.

The volunteer cleared her throat quickly. "Well, she is considered a senior but don't let her age fool you. She's still got plenty of spirit left in her."

Aiden crouched beside me and studied the dog. "She's cute."

"Her name is Daisy," I said.

"Hello, Daisy." He stuck his fingers between the bars and Daisy sniffed at them before turning her warm brown eyes to me again.

"How old is she?" Aiden asked.

"She's eleven but again, she's in reasonably good health for her age and it's always been my opinion that an older dog is a much better pet than a puppy."

There was an odd note of desperation in the volunteer's voice and Aiden frowned at me. I shrugged a little as the volunteer said, "Would you like to go into the kennel and pet her?"

"Sure," I said.

We stood and the volunteer opened the kennel and the three of us slipped inside. Daisy's tail wagged and she brushed up against me before sitting politely. I crouched again and rubbed her side. Her tail wagged harder and she leaned her stocky body against mine. I would have fallen over if Aiden hadn't steadied me before crouching next to us.

"She's a sweet little thing," he said.

"Yes, but she's eleven," I pointed out. "I'm not sure I want a senior dog again. I wouldn't have many years with her."

"Pit Bulls can live to be fifteen," the volunteer said brightly. "I have a friend who has a pitty who is almost seventeen."

She scratched around Daisy's ears and the dog panted happily at her. "She really is very lovely. You won't have any behaviour issues with her."

"I like her," Aiden said. He scratched Daisy's rump and she made a harrumph of pleasure before standing and sitting next to him. He stroked her head and grinned at me.

"I'm only supposed to be looking today," I reminded him. "I'm leaving Thursday for the weekend, remember?"

"I'll look after her," he said. "I don't mind."

He glanced at the volunteer. "Does she get along well with other dogs?"

"Oh, you have another dog?" The volunteer said.

"No," I said, "I don't have – "

"Yes," Aiden interrupted me. "We have a one-year-old English Mastiff. He's good with other dogs."

"Well, you can bring your dog to the shelter and do a meet and greet with Daisy," the woman said. "That's no problem."

"He's in our car. Could we have them meet today?" He asked.

She nodded. "Absolutely. In fact, I was going to suggest bringing him today."

"Aiden," I said, "She's a senior dog and with that comes – "

"There's a red tag on the front of her kennel. What does that mean?" Aiden asked abruptly.

The woman's smile slipped a little. "She's scheduled to be put down tomorrow."

My heart dropped and I stared wide-eyed at Aiden as he frowned at the woman. "Why?"

"Not because she's a bad dog," the woman said hastily. "She really isn't. It's just, well, she's a Pit Bull and she's older and she's been here for a while."

I stared into Daisy's warm brown eyes as the volunteer continued, "The stigma about Pit Bulls being dangerous isn't true. They're actually very loving and friendly dogs with people and other animals. Daisy doesn't have a mean bone in her body. It's such a shame that she's been looked over because of her breed and her age. I could give you plenty of website links that give you information on what the breed is actually like. Why don't I – "

"That won't be necessary," I interrupted and the woman sighed in resignation before patting Daisy's head.

"Can you get King from the car?" I asked Aiden.

He grinned delightedly and helped me stand as the volunteer clapped her hands. For one brief moment I thought she was going to hug me and I smiled at her as she settled for patting my arm awkwardly.

"We'll take Daisy into meeting room three," she said. "Just tell the volunteer at the front what room and she'll bring you there with your dog, okay?"

Aiden nodded and gave me a quick kiss before leaving. The volunteer slipped a lead around Daisy's thick neck and we walked slowly down the hall.

* * *

"Aiden, you bought too much stuff."

"I didn't buy too much stuff."

"You did," I laughed. "I need to pay you for it."

"Nope, consider it a welcome home gift to Daisy."

I smiled and stared at the large pile of treats and toys piled on the top of my kitchen table. Daisy, a new bright pink collar around her neck, was sniffing the room curiously. King, his tongue lolling, was following closely behind and there was no mistaking the look of adoration he was giving her. When she stopped to investigate Rex's empty food dish, King licked at her face enthusiastically.

"King," Aiden sighed, "try and make her work for it a little, would you?"

I laughed as Daisy wandered out of the kitchen and down the hallway, King at her heels. "At least he likes her. Maybe they could have play dates every once in a while."

Aiden kissed my forehead. "It's almost dinner. Do you want to go out and eat or stay in?"

"Probably better if we stay in," I said. "I'm not sure King and Daisy are ready to be on their own together yet."

He nodded and opened the fridge before rummaging through it. God, it was getting way too easy to think of this as a relationship. He was making it easy and I had to work hard to tamp down the thread of hope that was building inside of me.

Aiden doesn't do relationships. Don't ever forget that.

"Aiden, after dinner I think it's probably best if you – "

"After dinner," he said as he pulled out a bag of salad. "I'm going to take you to bed and fuck your brains out, Lina."

I laughed. "I hate to tell you this, but that happened last night. In fact, I'm not entirely sure I've fully recovered."

He set the salad on the counter. "I'll go easy on you tonight. Maybe just regular orgasms instead of g-spot orgasms."

"How kind of you," I said. "What do you think of teriyaki chicken for dinner?"

"Sounds good," he replied. "I'm going to go check on the lovebirds."

He left the kitchen and I took out the chicken and popped it into the microwave to defrost. Faintly, I could hear Aiden talking to the dogs and I closed my eyes and rubbed briefly at my forehead.

You're playing a dangerous game, Lina.

Yeah, tell me something I don't know.

* * *

"Lina?"

"Yeah?"

I curled into Aiden's warm embrace. I was sleepy after my orgasms and ready to go to sleep but Aiden sounded wide awake. I had meant to ask him to leave after sex but damn if it didn't feel good to be in his arms. Besides, it was dark and cold and snowing. It would be downright rude of me to ask him to leave after he had fucked me into my current stupor.

"I was thinking maybe I would go with you to your sister's this weekend."

I sat up in a hurry, my sleepiness gone in an instant, and stared blankly at him. "What?"

He grinned at me. "It would be nice to have a weekend away."

"Aiden, I…"

I trailed off and stared at Daisy and King. The two of them were crammed on to Rex's old bed and King had his head resting on Daisy's hip. The both of them were snoring loudly and as Aiden sat up and took my hand, I realized I was utterly and completely furious with him.

"We can take the dogs to Joe's and Steph's. They wouldn't mind looking after them for the weekend," he said. "We could – "

"What are you doing?" I interrupted.

"What do you mean?"

"You were very clear that you didn't do relationships, that this was a fuck buddy thing only, and now you want to go to my sister's with me?"

A scowl crossed his face. "I've taken fuck buddies on weekend getaways before, Lina. It doesn't mean we're in a relationship."

"This isn't a weekend getaway, Aiden," I snapped. "This is going to meet my goddamn family. Is this some sort of game to you? Is that it?"

"What the hell is that supposed to mean?" He said. "Suddenly I'm a bad guy for wanting to spend time with you?"

"No, you're a bad guy for making me think that this is more than just sex," I said. "You're fixing things in my house, you're bringing me dinner and watching movies with me, you're spending the weekend and you're picking out a goddamn dog with me. What the hell, Aiden? We had a very clear agreement on what this was and I don't appreciate you changing the rules now. And if this is some sick little game for you – that's just fucked-up. You've told me repeatedly that you don't do relationships. Have you forgotten that?"

"You're right," he said abruptly. He climbed out of the bed and began to dress. "I apologize, Lina. I'm acting inappropriately and it won't happen again."

I was still furious and I glared at him as he buttoned his shirt. "You need to make a decision, Aiden. Are we in a relationship or am I just one more notch in your bedpost?"

He stiffened, his hands clenching into fists, and stared at the floor. "We're not in a relationship."

"Then stop being so goddamn nice to me!" I shouted stupidly.

"No problem," he snapped. He whistled for King and the dog raised his head and made a snort of displeasure.

"King, now," he snapped again and with a weary sigh, King heaved his body up and lumbered to Aiden.

"Good night, Ms. Jones," he said icily.

"Good night, Mr. Wright," I replied.

He left the bedroom with King, shutting the door hard behind him and I collapsed on the bed and stared silently at the ceiling. I kept it together until I heard the front door slam and then burst into tears.

* * *

"Lina, honey, don't take this the wrong way but you look like shit," Amanda said solemnly.

I smiled faintly. "Thanks."

"Tell me what's wrong."

"Nothing's wrong," I said. "I'm just tired."

"Maybe you should take tomorrow off," Amanda suggested. "Get some rest."

"I can't. I'm already taking Friday off to visit my sister. I leave tomorrow night."

"That's right, I forgot," Amanda replied before biting into her banana. "You must be looking forward to it."

"You have no idea," I sighed before stirring my yogurt. I had no appetite and I pushed it aside before taking a drink of water.

"Is it Mr. Wright?" Amanda asked suddenly.

I gave her a startled look. "What do you mean?"

"Is he being a dickhead again? I thought he was getting better after you threatened to quit but hey, a leopard doesn't change his spots, right?"

"No, it has nothing to do with him," I lied. "I'm just not sleeping well."

That part wasn't a lie. I hadn't slept well since my epic orgasm Saturday night. I wished bitterly that I had kept my mouth shut on Sunday, that I had just found a polite way to tell Aiden he couldn't go with me to Kate's. God, I missed him.

He's done with you, girl. Move on.

Yeah, he was. He had been polite and professional at work for the last three days and that was it. I had resolved to keep my distance, to let Aiden decide if and when he wanted to have sex again, but already that resolve was wavering. I had nearly texted him last night after dinner, a quick and I thought brilliantly casual message asking if he wanted to get together. Instead, I had deleted the message, grabbed Daisy's leash and took her for as long of a walk as she could handle.

Thank God for Daisy. She was an absolute sweetheart of a dog and while she would never replace Rex in my heart, after only three days she had wagged her way into her own permanent spot. If it hadn't been for her, I would probably have cracked and contacted Aiden.

Yes, because who wouldn't want to be rejected for sex by their hot-as-sin boss? Jesus, Lina, you had your chance and you fucking blew it. You should have kept your big mouth shut and just left it alone. You were seeing things that weren't there, blowing his small gestures of kindness way out of control, and now you've paid the price for it. He's finished with you. Just like I said he would be.

I wanted to reach into my skull and tear my inner voice right out of my head.

Unaware of my inner turmoil, Amanda said, "How is Daisy doing?"

"Good. She acts like she's lived with me forever," I said with a small smile. "No accidents in the house and I'm slowly figuring out what commands she knows. I need to get her checked out by my vet when I come back from Kate's. She's pretty stiff in the morning and I think could benefit from some glucosamine but she's such a happy, sweet girl. I love her already."

"Good. What are you doing with her while you're gone?"

"Oh, uh, I've got a friend looking after her," I replied.

I had actually been panicking a little, unsure if Aiden would still keep his promise to look after Daisy, but that fear had been alieved earlier this morning. He had sent me a brief email, asking if I could drop Daisy at his place around seven tonight, and I had breathed a sigh of relief before sending a quick reply.

"Lina?" Amanda asked again. "Are you sure you're okay? You know you can talk to me, right?"

"I do," I said and forced a smile on my face. I liked Amanda but there was no way I was talking to her about fucking my boss. Hell, I couldn't even bring myself to tell Tracy that Aiden was over me. It was like a small part of me couldn't stop hoping that Aiden would want to continue for just a little longer. It hadn't been a month, after all.

God, could you be more pathetic, Lina.

I smiled again at Amanda. "Seriously, everything is fine. Stop worrying."

* * *

The elevator doors slid open and I stepped into Aiden's penthouse. He was waiting for me and despite my anxiety, I couldn't stop my smile when King saw Daisy. He woofed happily and bounded toward her, his tail wagging and drool flying from his mouth. He licked her face eagerly before pawing at her and Daisy nudged him with her big head.

"Someone's happy to see her," I said.

"He's missed her," Aiden said gruffly.

"She's missed him too," I replied quietly.

There was an awkward moment of silence before I cleared my throat and held out the large bag I was carrying. "So, here's her food and her dishes and toys. I forgot to bring her bed."

"That's fine. I have a feeling King will happily give up his bed for her," Aiden said as he took the bag and set it on the floor.

I smiled a little. "Probably. I'm back Sunday night at six but I'll need to go home first and grab my car. Is eight too late to pick her up?"

He shook his head and I hesitated before smiling tentatively at him. "Thank you again for looking after her. If you have any problems, just text me, okay?"

"I will. Enjoy your visit with your sister."

"Thanks," I replied. I knelt down, pushing King and his enthusiastic licking aside, and scratched Daisy's forehead before giving her a brief hug. "Bye, Daisy. I'll be back in a few days. Be good for Aiden."

She nudged my hand and I pressed a kiss against her head before standing and giving Aiden another tentative smile. "Bye, Aiden. Have a nice weekend."

"You too, Lina."

I pushed the elevator button and the doors opened immediately. A part of me had hoped that Aiden would ask me to stay for a while. That our fight from Sunday would be forgiven and forgotten and he would take me to his bed. It had been a ridiculous thing to hope for, I knew that, but now that it was obvious, I was feeling horribly depressed and close to tears. I blinked them back fiercely – I would not cry in front of Aiden – and stepped into the elevator.

I squealed in surprise when my arm was grabbed and I was yanked back into the apartment. Aiden, his face a mask of need and something else I couldn't identify, pushed me against the wall and kissed me. His hand tangled in my hair, holding me tightly, as he thrust his tongue into my mouth and kissed me with a desperate need.

I returned his kisses frantically and when his hands tore at the button to my jeans, I returned the favour. I raked his pants and underwear down his legs and reached for his cock. He was hard and huge and oh God, I had missed this - missed him.

I kicked off my shoes as Aiden pushed my jeans and my panties down to my ankles. I shook them off impatiently while Aiden kneaded my breasts through my t-shirt and bra. He was still kissing me, deep forceful kisses that made my core ache and my body shudder. I made a short noise of protest when he grabbed my naked ass and lifted me.

"Aiden, wait. You're going to hurt yourself. Don't - "

He kissed me again, cutting off my protests as he shoved his body between my naked thighs. His cock brushed against my clit and he shifted me higher before thrusting his cock deep into my pussy.

I wasn't quite ready for him and I moaned at the exquisite combination of pleasure edged with just a hint of pain as my body tried to adjust to the unexpected invasion. Aiden swore under his breath and pinned my lower half to the wall before reaching between us and rubbing at my clit. It didn't take long before I was wet and he gripped my ass with both hands again and thrust back and forth. I stared wildly at him, my chest heaving as I gasped for air and my legs clinging tightly to his narrow hips.

"Touch yourself," he demanded.

I rubbed my clit as he slammed in and out, my back hitting the wall with muffled, rhythmic thuds. I was soaking wet now and he drove in and out with ease as my cries of pleasure grew louder.

"You belong to me," he suddenly said. "Say it."

I stared wide-eyed at him, my hand slowing to a stop. "Aiden, I – "

He stopped his wild thrusting, pinning me to the wall with his hard cock, and snarled angrily, "You belong to me, Lina Jones. You're mine! Say it!"

"I belong to you," I whispered.

"Again."

"I belong to you, Aiden."

"Always," he muttered before thrusting again. I cried out with pleasure and resumed my frantic rubbing at my clit.

"Come for me, princess," he whispered into my ear and I shattered around him. I made a high keening noise as he groaned loudly and thrust a final time before joining me in climaxing. We shook against each other and I clutched him tightly as he buried his face in my neck.

When he lowered me to the floor, my legs were weak from the aftershocks of my orgasm and he steadied me before pulling up his pants and taking my hand. Without speaking, he led me to the bedroom and stripped me of the rest of my clothes before helping me into his bed. He undressed and joined me, sliding his arm around my waist and cupping my breast.

"Did I hurt you, Lina?" He asked.

I shook my head. "No. Why would you think that?"

He sighed. "I was rough and you weren't ready for me. I'm sorry."

"It's fine," I said. "I'm not hurt."

He kissed the back of my shoulder and I relaxed in his embrace for nearly half an hour before I tugged at his arm. "Let me go."

He tightened his grip and I patted his arm lightly. "I can't stay, Aiden."

"I miss you," he whispered.

"I miss you too but it still isn't a good idea for me to stay."

"You said you belonged to me," he said in a low voice. "Did you mean it or was it just something I forced you to say?"

"I meant it," I said quietly.

He turned me over to face him and searched my face anxiously. I cupped his cheek and stroked his mouth before smiling at him. "I belong to you."

He buried his face in my throat and kissed the soft skin.

"I want to try, Lina." His voice was muffled and I tugged lightly until he lifted his head.

"Try what?" I asked.

"Try dating, being in a relationship with you," he said.

I stared in shocked silence at him and he sighed loudly. "Fuck, it's too late isn't it? I blew it."

I shook my head and pressed a kiss against his mouth. "It isn't too late."

"I'll probably suck at it," he said.

I laughed, "I'll keep that in mind."

"I'd prefer if people at the office didn't know," he said cautiously. "At least for now."

"You and me both," I replied.

For a brief moment I considered asking him why he had changed his mind before deciding it didn't matter. I wanted to be with Aiden and he wanted to be with me. Nothing else mattered.

* * *

"Wait, so first you were just sleeping with your boss as a casual thing but now you're dating?" Kate popped a piece of sushi into her mouth before pointing her chopsticks at me. "Who are you and what have you done with my baby sister?"

"What do you mean?" I laughed.

"Lina, this isn't you. First you're having a fling with the guy who writes your paycheque and now you're going to date him? You know how dangerous this is, right? What if it doesn't work and he fires you?"

"He wouldn't do that," I said firmly. "Trust me, Kate. I know what I'm doing."

"Do you?" She asked.

"Yes."

"Are you in love with him?"

I hesitated and her light green eyes widened. "Holy shit, you are."

"I might be," I said.

"Does he love you?"

"I doubt it." I made my voice light-hearted. "And that's fine."

She frowned at me and I ate a piece of sushi before smiling at her. "It is, Kate. I want to be with him and he wants to be with me. That makes me happy."

"For now," she said.

"For now," I agreed. "Enough about me. How is work going? Gerald still being a pain in your ass?"

She blinked at me. "I didn't tell you."

"Tell me what?"

"Gerald passed away."

"What? When? How?"

"He was playing golf two weeks ago and had a heart attack."

"Oh my gosh, that's terrible."

"It is," she said. "We had our difficulties when I first started working for him but we had worked them out and he was a surprisingly good boss."

She tugged at a lock of her flame-coloured hair. "I thought for sure I was going to lose my job, it's hard to be a personal assistant to a non-existent partner in a law firm, but Arthur called me into his office on Thursday and assured me that I still had a job. They've brought in a new partner, Edward something or other. He starts next week."

"Well, that's good, I guess."

She nodded. "I'm thankful to still have a job but I'm hoping that this Edward guy is a little more easy going than Gerald was. At the very least, I'm hoping he'll get his own damn coffee."

"Maybe he'll be young and handsome," I teased. "Then you'll know exactly what I'm going through."

She laughed. "No, thanks. One – unlike your company we have a very strict policy on inter-office dating and two – even if we were allowed to date our coworkers there's no way in hell I'm getting involved with my boss. That's just asking for trouble."

She paused before saying, "No offense."

"None taken," I said.

"Besides, there's a super cute guy on the train that I've been flirting with for the last few weeks."

"Ooh, give me the details," I said.

"There's not much at the moment. His name is Josh and he's a financial consultant. He's got dark hair and hazel eyes and he's about my height."

"Sounds promising."

"I think so," Kate replied as a fat grey-coloured tabby wandered into the kitchen.

As it brushed past me, I reached down and stroked its back. It hissed balefully at me before swiping at me with its claws and flouncing from the kitchen."

"I see Chicken is as friendly as ever."

Kate laughed. "She's complicated."

I rolled my eyes before eating the last of my sushi. "What time are mom and dad getting here?"

"Around three. Dad had to work this morning but he was finishing up early so they could beat the traffic. Are you going to tell them about Aiden?"

I shook my head. "No, not yet so keep it to yourself, okay?"

"I will. Olivia wants the four of us to come over around three on Saturday. Apparently Jon is barbequing."

"You know there are perks to living in California in the winter," I laughed. "Barbequing in the middle of January being one of them."

Kate grinned at me. "Mom and dad are having coffee with the Rickards tonight. Are we hitting the bar or what?"

"I'm up for it if you are. Maybe you should invite Josh."

Kate shook her head. "I don't even have his number yet."

She leaned forward and took my hand. "Lina, are you sure you want to date your boss? This is real life, not some romance novel, and this kind of thing rarely works out."

"I'm sure," I said. "Stop worrying, Katie-did. It's going to be just fine."

Chapter 15

I scanned the crowd of people standing at the arrival gate a little nervously. Before I'd left, Aiden had offered to pick me up from the airport and I had gratefully accepted. Friday and Saturday we had texted off and on and Saturday night I had called him after Kate had gone to bed, just to chat. Everything had seemed fine but today I hadn't heard from him at all.

Relax, Lina. You're not joined at the hip for God's sake. He was probably working.

Yes, probably. But it didn't stop the little niggle of worry that was growing in my belly. The worry grew when I finally spotted Aiden. He looked tired and upset and I hurried toward him.

"Hi, Lina."

He gave me a brief hug and a peck to the cheek. I frowned at him when he stepped away from my embrace.

"Hi. What's wrong?"

"Nothing," he said. "Do you need to pick up any luggage?"

"No," I replied. "I just have a carry-on."

He took the heavy bag and slung it over his shoulder. "Daisy and King are waiting in the car."

I took his hand and he squeezed it briefly before dropping it. My worry turned into full-blown anxiety as we walked silently out of the airport.

* * *

"Aiden, please tell me what's wrong," I said quietly. We were standing in my kitchen and Aiden was watching blankly as Daisy and King padded in circles around me. Both their tails were wagging and I winced and pulled my foot free when King sat on it.

The drive home from the airport has been filled with thick, tense silence and not even Daisy's obvious excitement at seeing me could break it.

"I can't help you if you won't tell me what's going on," I said.

"My father called me this morning. He and my mother have separated again and this time, they're getting a divorce."

"I'm sorry," I said. I pushed past the dogs and wrapped my arms around Aiden's waist. "I'm so sorry, honey."

"I asked my father if he had cheated on her again," he said dully. "He didn't get angry, he just said that he had been faithful to her and that he still loved her and didn't want the divorce. I didn't believe him."

He suddenly laughed bitterly and pushed his way free of my embrace. "I called my mom and – you'll love this part – it turns out that she's been cheating on him. Has been for the last two years. She and her lover are moving in together, are getting married. She said it wasn't a retaliation for what happened years ago but I know that isn't true. She never really forgave him."

"Aiden." I tried to take his hand and he shook his head before backing away.

"This isn't going to work, Lina."

"What?" I whispered.

"Us. Dating, having a relationship. I was a fucking idiot to think it would."

"Aiden, stop," I said. "What's happened with your parents is terrible and I'm sorry for you, but I'm not your mother and you're not your father. Just because their relationship is dysfunctional and broken, doesn't mean that ours will be."

He didn't reply and, fear blooming in my belly, I gripped his arms tightly. "You're not a teenager anymore. You're a grown man who is intelligent enough to know that every relationship is different. Don't give up on ours just because your parents' isn't working."

"We'll end up hurting each other," he said. "Maybe not because of cheating or lying but there'll be something that destroys our happiness. And then we'll both be alone and miserable."

"That's not true," I said. "Plenty of couples are happy. It takes work and I can't promise you that it'll always be sunshine and ice cream, but love is never easy. If it was, there wouldn't – "

"Are you in love with me?" He interrupted.

"Yes," I said. "I am."

Confusion, mixed with anger and helplessness, crossed his face. I tried to cup his face and he jerked away from me.

"Don't, Lina. I have to go."

"Please don't walk away from me," I said.

"I have to," he said. "I don't want to hurt you. Don't you understand that?"

"You're hurting me now," I said quietly. "Don't you understand *that*?"

"I'm sorry, Lina," he said hoarsely. "But I can't be with you. It's over."

He whistled for King and I watched numbly as the man I loved walked away.

* * *

"Daisy? C'mon, girl, get your lazy bones out of bed."

Daisy yawned and stretched stiffly as I sat on the bed and pulled on my boots. She gave me a reproachful look as I stood.

"I know it's early but it'll do us both some good to go for a walk. Let's go, girl."

She followed me slowly out of the bedroom and to the front door. It had been a week since Aiden had broken my heart and other than not sleeping, not eating and the random bursts of pathetic sobbing, I thought I was handling it okay. This morning I was even feeling like the depression that surrounded me in a thick shroud had lifted a little.

"Of course," I said to Daisy as I zipped up my jacket and grabbed her leash, "that's probably because I only have a week left of seeing Aiden every single fucking day. And, listen, I know you had a little affair going on with King but trust me — it's better for you not to see him. When the weather warms up I'll take you to the dog park and you can find yourself a new boyfriend."

I grabbed my keys, clipped Daisy's leash to her collar and stepped into the chilly air. It was just after seven and the sky was grey and dull. Daisy made a low whine of disapproval and I tugged gently on her collar.

"Get moving, lazy bones. I need to get in some exercise. My new job will have me moving a lot more and I don't want to be crippled after my first day."

Monday morning, I had immediately started looking for a new job. By that evening I had emailed seven resumes to various companies. To my surprise, the very first place I had sent my resume to – a large industrial factory that was looking for an assistant for their warehouse manager – had contacted me Tuesday afternoon. We had set up an interview for early Wednesday morning and when Dan, the warehouse manager, had offered me the job on the spot, I had accepted. Dan was pushing sixty and he had proudly shown me the picture of his wife on the bookshelf behind his desk before pulling out his phone so I could see the pictures of his granddaughter. I had liked him immediately, he had an easy-going manner that was completely different from Aiden's, and there was no chance in hell of falling in love with him.

"Not that I'm ever going to fall in love with a boss again, Daisy," I puffed as we walked quickly down the sidewalk. "I don't care if he's a goddamn movie star with more money than God, I've learned my lesson."

I had placed my letter of resignation on Aiden's desk Thursday morning before he arrived at the office. He had a client meeting early that morning and by the time he got to the office around ten, my stomach was rolling from nerves and I could barely stop from throwing up. He had walked past me, greeting me politely without looking at me like he had done for the last three days, and disappeared into his office.

I had braced myself for his reaction, waiting for his voice to call me into his office. Would he be angry or happy? Would he try to convince me to stay? I had no damn idea and my legs were shaking so badly I was afraid I wouldn't even make it into his office. It turned out that I hadn't needed to be worried. Aiden didn't say a single word to me about the resignation letter. I would have wondered if he had even seen it if HR hadn't contacted me just after lunch to schedule my exit interview.

"I don't care," I said to Daisy as we turned the corner and headed back home. "I don't care that he doesn't care that I'm leaving. Aiden Wright is a dickhead and I'm better off without him."

Liar.

I blinked back the tears that were always so close to the surface now and walked a little faster. Yeah, I was full of fucking bullshit but if I didn't at least try and pretend it didn't matter, didn't pretend that I didn't miss Aiden so much it was killing me, I wouldn't have a chance of getting over him.

"I will be okay," I whispered to Daisy. "I'll get over it. It'll just take time."

Fifteen minutes later we were standing at the front door and I patted her head lightly before unlocking the door. I slipped off my shoes and unclipped her leash. She wandered down the hallway and disappeared into the kitchen as I hung my jacket on the hook.

"I'm just going to have a quick shower and get ready for work and then you can have your breakfast," I called after her. "Be a good girl and don't get into trouble while I'm – "

Daisy's low growling made my voice die in my throat. I had never once heard her growl and I knew instinctively that something was wrong. My heart thudding in my chest, I ran down the hallway and into the kitchen.

"Daisy? What's wrong? Why are you..."

I trailed off, staring in shock at the man standing in my kitchen. It was cold in the room, the hole smashed in the glass pane of the back door was letting in the cold air, and my eyes widened when the man dropped my laptop to the floor and yanked a knife from the block on the counter.

He was dressed in thin pants and a dirty and torn red jacket with a baseball cap pulled low on his head. His face and ears were bright red with the cold and, as his gaze darted from me to Daisy, even from across the kitchen I could see the way his pupils were blown out.

Drugs, Lina. He's high on something and that makes him very dangerous.

"We'll leave," I said shakily. "You can take whatever you want. Okay?"

"Bitch, you stay right the fuck where you are," he snarled at me. His hand clenched tightly on the handle of the knife and a sob of fear escaped my throat when he took a step toward me.

"You're going to give me your wallet and all of your jewelry or I will fuck you up. Do you hear me, bitch?"

I nodded and took a step back as the man advanced another step.

"Where the fuck do you think you're going?" The man suddenly shouted. "I told you not to fucking move."

He started toward me, raising the knife as he did. "You think I was fucking joking?" He shouted again. "You think I won't – "

I screamed shrilly when Daisy, snarling viciously, leaped at the man and bit him on the face. He shrieked in fear and pain and drove the knife into Daisy's side. She made a harsh cry of pain and fell to the floor with a horrid thud, and I screamed again as the man staggered back. Blood was pouring from his face and he stared wide-eyed at Daisy lying motionless at his feet before touching his torn and gaping cheek.

He turned, blood spraying from his face to land on the wall and counter, and fled out the back door. Crying loudly, I staggered to Daisy and dropped to my knees beside her body.

"Daisy? Oh, Daisy, oh, honey," I sobbed.

She was whimpering and whining quietly and, my arms were shaking so badly I could barely lift her. I staggered back under her heavy weight, struggling to keep my balance as Daisy made another loud whimper of pain.

"You'll be okay, honey. Mama's here, you'll be okay," I whispered as, my entire body shaking from the exertion, I lurched out of the kitchen and toward the front door.

* * *

"Good morning, Amanda speaking."

"Amanda, it's Lina. I need you to do me a favour."

"If it's picking you up a coffee, it's already done, my friend. Although it's probably cold by now. Are you running late? Do you need me to make up an excuse for Mr. Wr – "

"Amanda, listen to me!" I interrupted. "Can you tell Aiden that I – I won't be in until later today."

"Lina, honey, what's wrong?" Amanda said cautiously. "You sound upset."

"S-someone broke into my house this morning and – "

"Oh my God!"

"He, he tried to attack me and Daisy bit him but he stabbed her. I – I'm at the emergency vet with her right now. Can you let Aiden know I'll be late?" I was nearly sobbing into my cell phone and I grabbed a tissue from the box the receptionist was holding out to me and wiped at my streaming eyes as the emergency vet came striding into the reception area.

"Of course I can. Honey, are you okay? Did you get hurt or – "

"I have to go, Amanda," I said. "The vet needs to talk to me."

I hung up and, my heart in my throat, stared fearfully at the vet.

* * *

Thirty minutes later, as I sat in the hard chair and stared dully at my hands, the door to the emergency vet burst open and Aiden flew into the reception. He knelt at my feet and cupped my head.

"Lina! Lina, are you okay?"

He stared at the blood stained across my shirt. "Fuck, I'm taking you to the hospital right now."

"It's not my blood," I said bleakly. "It's Daisy's. I'm not hurt, Aiden."

He touched my face, my shoulders and my arms before cupping my head again. "What happened, honey?"

"How did you know where I was?" I asked sluggishly.

"I Googled the closest emergency vet to your house," he said patiently. "Tell me what happened, honey."

"I was taking Daisy for a walk and when we got home, there was a man in my kitchen. He-he had smashed the window in the back door. He had a knife and he- he started toward me and Daisy attacked him. She bit him in the face and he stabbed her with the knife and then she fell on the floor and then he ran."

I started to sob and Aiden sat beside me and scooped me into his lap. He stroked my hair and rocked me back and forth. "Shh, honey, it's okay. Shh."

"She saved my life," I sobbed. "She's in surgery and the vet s-said she h-has a fifty/fifty chance of s-surviving it."

"She'll be okay, honey," Aiden said soothingly. "She's a tough dog. She'll make it, Lina."

I threw my arms around him and clung tightly as he rubbed my back.

"I'm getting blood on you," I whispered.

"It doesn't matter, baby. All that matters is your safe," he murmured.

After a few minutes, he said, "Did you call the police?"

"No, I just – just picked up Daisy and took her straight to the emergency vet. I didn't even think to call the police."

"That's okay. I'll take care of it."

"Thank you," I whispered.

He hugged me closely before sliding me off his lap and on to the chair. "I'll just be a few minutes."

* * *

"Ms. Jones, are you sure you don't need to go to the hospital?" The police officer asked.

I nodded and he studied his notes before smiling at me. "Okay, I think we have everything we need. We've sent a unit to your house to dust for fingerprints and we've – "

"You should check the hospitals," Aiden interrupted. "If the bite is as deep as Lina says it was, then he'll need medical treatment."

"We already have someone calling the hospitals," the officer replied. "Don't worry, Ms. Jones, we'll find him. In the meantime, you might want to think of staying somewhere else over the weekend. I doubt he'll come back but it's probably better for you not to be there alone."

"She's staying with me," Aiden said. "She's not staying in that house ever again."

A little of the fog lifted from my brain and I blinked at him. "Aiden, it's my home. I can't just leave and never go back."

"We'll talk about it later," he said firmly before standing and shaking the officer's hand. "Thanks for your help. You have my cell number, call me as soon as you find this guy."

I barely heard the officer's reply. The vet had come into reception and, dread building in my belly, I stood and stared at his grave face.

"Is she dead?" I asked hoarsely as Aiden slipped his arm around my waist.

"No," the vet said kindly. "In fact, all things considered, she did fairly well."

I sagged against Aiden and started to cry as the vet smiled at me. "She's not out of the woods yet. We're going to keep her over the weekend and monitor her progress but I think she has a good prognosis for recovery."

"Can I see her?" I whispered.

"Yes. She's not awake from surgery yet but you can see her now and then, if you'd like, you can come by tomorrow morning. She'll be more awake then. If there are any problems, we'll call you, okay?"

I nodded, still crying softly, and grabbed the vet's hand. "Thank you so much."

"You're welcome, Ms. Jones. Follow me."

* * *

"Lina?"

"I'm still in the tub," I called. I sunk lower into the water as Aiden entered the bathroom.

"How are you feeling?" He asked anxiously.

"A little better," I said. "Thanks for letting me use your tub."

"You're welcome."

"How – how did it go?"

"It was fine. I cleaned up the blood and nailed a board over the smashed window. It's not pretty but it works for now. I'll replace the glass next weekend and start working on the other repairs so you can get the house ready for sale."

"Aiden," I said, "I can't sell my house just because – "

"I grabbed some clothes and your toiletries, enough for the weekend," he interrupted.

"Thank you. I appreciate that," I said. "Listen, I can stay at Tracy's. It's really nice of you to let me stay here but Tracy has an extra bedroom and – "

"You're staying right here with me," he interrupted again. "This isn't a topic for discussion. Do you understand?"

I nodded and he checked his cell phone.

"What time is it?"

"Almost one," he said. "Why?"

"I should get to the office," I said. "Can I get a ride with you? My car is still at the emergency vet."

"Neither of us are going into the office today," he said firmly. "You're going to have something to eat and then have a nap."

"I'm not hungry," I said. "I know you're busy at the office and you don't need to sit at home and babysit me. I'm perfectly fine."

He shook his head. "Again, not a topic for discussion."

I scrunched a little further down in the water. "Aiden, are you angry with me?"

"For what?" He asked.

"For quitting."

"No," he said quietly. "I know why you resigned and I understand."

I swallowed the lump in my throat as he sighed and said, "Do you have another job?"

"Yeah."

"What's your new boss like?"

I smiled a little. "He's sixty years old, Aiden."

A brief look of relief crossed his face. "Good."

He hesitated for a moment before saying, "The police called me. They found the guy. He was at St. Augustine's Hospital being treated for a dog bite. They arrested him but you'll have to go in and identify him in a line up."

I blew my breath out in a relieved rush as Aiden watched me carefully. "Thank God."

"I'll go with you to the station, okay?"

"Yes, thank you," I said. I sat up in the tub, crossing my arms over my naked breasts. "I think I've been in here long enough. Can you pass me the towel?"

Aiden unfolded the large towel and held it open. "Stand up, Lina."

"Um, I don't think – "

"I've seen you naked before," he reminded me gently. I sighed and stood. "I know."

He wrapped the towel around my wet body and lifted me out of the tub. His hands lingered on my upper chest as he tucked the towel and I made a soft moan when he dipped his head and placed a warm kiss against my wet skin. He lifted his gaze to mine and my body responded to the hunger and the need in his eyes.

"I'm sorry, Lina," he said hoarsely. "I shouldn't have done that."

He turned to leave and I grabbed his arm. "Aiden, please. I need you."

I stood on my tiptoes and kissed his neck. "Please," I whispered, "take me to bed."

"Are you sure?" He groaned. "I don't want to take advantage of you."

"You're not," I said. "I promise you're not."

I took his hand and tugged him out of the bathroom and into his bedroom. I dropped the towel, smiling at Aiden's sharp inhale, and quickly undressed him. I kissed his chest and stroked his cock until it was hard and throbbing in my hand before starting to kneel in front of him.

He shook his head and lifted me to my feet. "No, honey. I want to taste you."

I relaxed on the bed and spread my legs as Aiden stretched out between them. He kissed the top of my pussy before licking the crease of my thigh and I curled my hands into his hair and tugged him toward my aching core.

"I've missed you," he breathed against me before licking my clit.

I moaned and arched into his mouth as he licked me with infinite gentleness before sucking and nibbling my clit. It didn't take long for me to climax, I had missed him just as much, and he knelt between my thighs and entered me with a slow stroke while I was still shaking and moaning from my orgasm.

I let my legs fall apart and squeezed his ass as he moved in a slow and gentle rhythm that made me yearn for more.

"Harder, Aiden," I whispered.

"No," he said. "Not yet, honey."

"Please," I begged.

He kissed me softly, licking the curve of my upper lip before sucking on my bottom one. I slipped my tongue into his mouth, tears starting to slide down my face at his familiar taste and he kissed them away.

"Don't cry, honey."

He cupped my breast, teasing and tugging on my nipple as I moaned and dug my fingers into his back.

I closed my eyes and he pressed a kiss against each of my eyelids. "Open your eyes, Lina. Look at me."

I held his gaze as he stopped moving. He kissed me lightly before saying, "When Amanda told me someone had broken into your house, when I didn't know if you were hurt or not – I almost went crazy. It made me realize what a goddamn idiot I was and that I needed to be with you. That I couldn't live without you."

I kissed his jaw and rubbed his back before rocking my pelvis against him. He groaned and smoothed my hair back from my face.

"I love you, Lina."

I swallowed compulsively and stared wide-eyed at him as he pressed a kiss against my mouth.

"I love you," he said again. "I'm so sorry for hurting you. I love you."

"I love you too," I said before cupping his face. "You belong to me."

He smiled and whispered, "I belong to you."

Epilogue

Two months later

"Lina? Where are you?"

"In here," I called. I threw another shirt into the suitcase as Aiden, pulling his tie loose, entered the bedroom. Daisy and King were weaving eagerly around his legs and he cursed as he tripped over Daisy and nearly fell.

Daisy barked and head butted him and he patted her head affectionately. "For being stabbed and nearly dying, she's remarkably nimble."

I laughed. "She's a tough dog, remember?"

He shrugged out of his suit jacket and hung it in the closet. "How was work?"

"Fine, a bit slow. Dan's daughter went into labour at eleven and he left for the hospital. He called me just before four – he has a new grandson."

"That's nice," Aiden said. He squeezed my ass affectionately and I handed him a t-shirt and a pair of jeans.

"Hurry up and change. I want to get up to the cabin before seven. Steph is waiting on dinner for us. How was your day?"

"Good. Parker's been flirting with my assistant."

I grinned. "I'm not surprised. He seems to have a thing for your assistants."

He growled playfully at me before slapping my ass. "He still flirts with you."

"No, he doesn't," I said. "Hugging me when I dropped by the office earlier this week is not flirting. Oh hey – the sale for the house went through today. I am officially homeless."

He sat down on the bed and pulled me into his lap, nuzzling my neck affectionately. "You're not homeless. You live with me, remember?"

"Well you never officially asked me to move in," I said tartly. "You just started moving my stuff in on a daily basis."

He grinned. "Asking you might have given you the impression that it was a choice. You belong to me, remember?"

"How could I forget. You won't let me have a damn orgasm until I say it," I said with a mock scowl.

"You like it," he said smugly. "You find me utterly irresistible."

"Utterly," I said.

"Sarcasm will get you a spanking," he said.

"Later," I said before kissing him. "We need to get to the cabin, remember?"

I slid off his lap, pausing when he squeezed my hand. "Lina?"

"Yeah?"

"It's good, isn't it? What's happening between us?"

"Yes," I said. "It's not always going to be easy, no relationship ever is, but I love you, Aiden, and I will never let you go."

He pulled me into his embrace. "I love you too, Ms. Jones."

END

Please enjoy a sample of Ramona's newest novel, "One Night".

"One Night" will be available in June of 2016.

"Oh darling," he murmured tenderly into her ear, "Until this very moment with you in my arms, I didn't realize just how empty my life was."

Kate smiled and lifted her face.

"Show me just how much you love me," she whispered.

His mouth was warm on hers and as he rained soft kisses on her full lips, Kate pressed her body against his. He kissed her passionately and Kate tried to lose herself in the moment but was increasingly distracted by his facial hair. Did he have a beard before? She couldn't remember. She shook off the nagging feeling that something wasn't right and parted her lips further, eager to deepen the kisses. She tried to slowly slide her tongue into his mouth but was thwarted by a thick layer of his facial hair.

What the hell?

Kate tried to pull back but his facial hair was everywhere, in her mouth, up her nose - she couldn't breathe. She was about to be the first woman in history to die of asphyxiation from facial hair. Before she could succumb to death by beard, the loud beeping of her alarm clock jarred her awake.

"Chicken, get off me!" She complained, her voice muffled by the 14lbs of cat currently lying across her head.

When Chicken refused to budge, Kate made the error of touching her. She had adopted Chicken from the local animal shelter three years ago. She had gone in with the expectation of adopting a cute, fluffy kitten with big eyes and long hair and who would charm everyone with her sweet personality and beautiful looks. An hour later she left with an old, fat grey tabby named Chicken whose personality was described by one volunteer as "unexpectedly angry".

But, as she explained to her best friend Olivia over coffee the next day, "She was scheduled to be put down that day, how was I supposed to just walk away from her?"

"Why is your hand all bandaged like that? Olivia asked.

"Chicken's not so, how do you say it...friendly with people? She likes her space," Kate replied.

"And those big scratches down your leg?" Olivia pointed to the painful looking scratches that started at Kate's knee and ended just above her ankle.

"Oh that? Well, you know my chair by the window in the sun room?

"Yes," Olivia replied.

"Chicken's decided that's her chair now and when I tried to move her over so I could sit down and share it with her she got a little, eh, territorial. But I'm sure she'll be fine in the next few days. She's still traumatized from being on death row," Kate said cheerfully.

In the three years since then Kate and Chicken had arrived at an unspoken agreement. Chicken wouldn't use her as a shredding post if Kate didn't try to touch her unless specifically invited to. Kate also learned fairly quickly to warn her guests to avoid touching Chicken, resist from looking her in the eye and that it was, in fact, probably best to just refrain from looking in the general direction of the angry tabby.

This morning, however, her body's will to survive overrode her common sense and as Kate reached up and gave the cat a shove on the butt to get her moving, Chicken growled and flung herself off Kate's head with an irritated hiss.

"Ouch! Dammit, Chicken!" Kate cried.

She slammed her hand down on the alarm clock, silencing it's frantic beeping, and crawled out of bed to inspect the damage to her face.

"Nice," she muttered as she peered into the bathroom mirror.

Thanks to Chicken's quick exit and razor sharp nails she now had a bright red scratch down the middle of her forehead. She had been shamelessly flirting with Josh, the super cute guy from the train, for the past two weeks and she could only imagine how well the flirting would go with a giant scratch on her forehead.

Nearly an hour later Kate carefully weaved her way through the usual crowd of people on the train. Why she was even moving to the back of the train where her potential boyfriend usually sat, she wasn't sure. Her morning hadn't gotten any better with the realization that she really should have done some laundry yesterday instead of re-watching the first two seasons of 'The Walking Dead'. Her lack of clean clothes had left her no choice but to wear one of her least flattering pairs of pants with a white shirt that had seen a few too many accidental spins in the dryer and was now a bit too snug for work. The shirt cupped her full breasts and hugged her lean stomach and as she pushed past people she could feel the unwelcoming glances of a couple of the more lecherous type fellows who rode the train.

"Excuse me, please," she murmured as she squeezed past a lady in her fifties.

"Sorry," she muttered to the young guy whose foot she had just stepped on.

She was almost at the end of the train - she could see the back of Josh's head. Just a few more steps and she'd be there, prepared to flirt her way into a dinner and movie date. With a sudden jolt the train started to move and Kate was flung sideways. Her feet tangled together and she fell with a graceless heap into the lap of a well-dressed businessman sitting on one of the side seats, her head slamming against the back of the seat with a loud bang.

With an unladylike grunt, she sat up straight and tried to scramble from the man's lap but his hands were on her waist and he was holding her firmly against him.

"Are you okay?" His deep voice washed over her.

"I'm fine, I'm so sorry..." she started and then stopped as her breath caught in her throat.

She was very close to the man's face, kissing distance as her mom liked to say, and she had never seen eyes that blue before. Her eyes traveled over his face before she could stop herself. He had dark hair with a hint of gray at the temples, a proud aristocratic nose and a hard angular jaw. She was mesmerized by the fullness of his bottom lip and stared in fascination when he smiled briefly and she got a glimpse of straight white teeth. She realized abruptly that she was still sitting on his lap and tried again to struggle her way free but he refused to let her go. He was saying something to her but her newly acquired head injury and the closeness of his warm, solid body seemed to have temporarily short circuited her brain.

"I didn't hear - what?" She stammered, still staring at his mouth.

"You've scratched your forehead on the seat," he said.

"What? Oh no, that's from Chicken in bed this morning," Kate mumbled.

"Chicken in bed?" The man arched one eyebrow and stared at her. "Do you mean you were eating chicken in bed or you share your bed with a chicken?"

"No! Chicken's my cat." Kate took a deep breath, her head had stopped ringing and she was aware of the bemused look on the faces of the other passengers around them. She was still sitting on the man's lap, his hands now placed firmly on her hips and their faces only inches apart.

"Really, I'm okay," Kate said, "I just need to stand up."

"Hold on," he said, "let me look at your head first."

Before Kate could protest he was holding her jaw with his lean fingers and turning her head to one side and then the other. He tugged gently on her chin, forcing her head down slightly. His other hand left her hip and as he slowly threaded his fingers through her thick red hair she wondered why it suddenly seemed so difficult to breathe. She winced when his fingers rubbed against the large scrape on her scalp.

"Sorry," he murmured into her ear, his warm breath sending shivers down her spine and a rush of heat to her lower body. "Looks like just a scrape, it's not bleeding."

He returned his hands to her hips. She ignored the butterflies in her stomach from the weight of his hands and cleared her throat.

"Please, let me up. I'm perfectly fine - just really embarrassed."

For the first time since she fell into his lap, the man seemed to really look at her. She could feel her face growing red as he stared at the scratch on her forehead. His astonishingly blue eyes looked briefly and intently into her light green ones and then moved lower to her mouth. Her mouth suddenly dry, Kate's lips parted slightly and her tongue darted out to wet her lower lip. He made a low noise in his throat at the sight of her tongue. With dawning horror, Kate felt her nipples harden when his gaze fell to her breasts. The snug white shirt left no doubt to the effect his bold look was having on her and when he glanced back up at her, his large hands tightening a little on her hips, she watched a slight grin cross his face for just a moment.

Angry at herself and her reaction to him, Kate placed her hands against his hard chest and shoved herself up and out of his arms as the train came to a bumpy stop.

"Thank you for your help," she said in a loud clear voice "but this is my stop".

She wobbled her way off the train, not caring that this was actually two stops early. She needed to get away from the intensity of his gaze and her body's shameful reaction to it. In the cool morning air, Kate held her aching head and took a few deep breaths as the train pulled away.

Everything is fine. Sure, you just fell into the lap of an incredibly handsome man and then humiliated yourself further by acting like some sex-starved maniac but you'll never see him again. Everything is cool.

"One Night" will be available in June 2016.

If you would like more information about Ramona Gray, please visit her at:

www.ramonagray.ca

or

https://www.facebook.com/RamonaGrayBooks

or

https://twitter.com/RamonaGrayBooks

Write to her at:

mailto:ramonagraybooks@gmail.com

Other books by Ramona Gray:

The Escort
Saving Jax
The Vampire's Kiss (Other World Series Book One)
The Vampire's Love (Other World Series Book Two)
The Shifter's Mate (Other World Series Book Three)
Rescued By The Wolf (Other World Series Book Four)